MY AUNT IS A PILOT WHALE

My Aunt
is a Pilot Whale

Anne Provoost

translated by Ria Bleumer

women's
P R E S S

CANADIAN CATALOGUING IN PUBLICATION DATA
Provoost, Anne, 1964—
        My aunt is a pilot whale

Translation of: Mijn tante is een grindewal.
ISBN 0-88961-202-1

I. Title.

PZ7.P76My 1994   j839.3'1364   C94-932445-0

Cover design: Christine Higdon
Cover art: Jody Hewgill
Revision and editing: Margaret Christakos

Published by Women's Press, 517 College Street, Suite 233,
Toronto, Ontario M6G 4A2

This book was produced by the collective effort of Women's Press and was a project of the Children's Literature Group.

Women's Press gratefully acknowledges the financial support of the Canada Council and the Ontario Arts Council.

Printed and bound in Canada
1 2 3 4 5   1998 1997 1996 1995 1994

1

Tara Myrold is my cousin. Her mother is my mother's sister. I haven't known her very long, because she and her parents used to live far away in Cleveland. Sometimes my mother would show me a picture of her, but she lived a day and a half's drive away, so I was never allowed to visit her.

A few years ago, we received a letter from Uncle Tony — his real name is Anton — saying they were coming to live with us in Cape Cod. Another picture of Tara was included and Mom let me have it. She said I should play a lot with Tara when she got here.

I held the photograph between two fingers and looked at it. I didn't think Tara was ugly or anything, just weird. She wore glasses and her hair was very thin, like she was already balding. She didn't smile and her blouse was crooked. I got the impression she didn't notice the photographer or the camera. Actually, it kind of looked as though she didn't really know what a photographer was. Her eyes didn't show up in the picture, because the light reflected off her glasses. Tara's face was in the picture but her thoughts were far away. That I could see clearly. I was nine then and I assumed Tara didn't have any thoughts.

I sniffed the picture. The paper smelled like washrooms and cigarettes. Tara seemed very dirty to me. She wore ugly red clothes and the strap of her undershirt showed on her shoulder. I could see that she rarely washed. I could also see that she sniffed instead of blowing her nose, because her face looked swollen. I put the picture between the wall and the cupboard in the garage and thought: I'll never play with Tara Myrold.

Dad didn't want Uncle Tony and Aunt Tanja to live with us either. He always said, "Anton is crazy," and actually meant "Tanja is crazy," but he didn't want to hurt Mom's feelings.

Mom's sister really was a little crazy. The whole family knew that. Sometimes she had to go to an institution because she was having a bad time, and sometimes she was at home.

"Their apartment in Cleveland is far too small. They only have one bedroom and a small kitchen. Tony says they can hear everything the neighbours say. And Tara wants to live by the ocean. If only they had more room, it would be easier for Aunt Tanja to go through her difficult times," said Mom.

"What do you mean 'difficult times?'" I asked.

"Times when she cries a lot, or forgets to cook dinner, or forgets to pick up Tara after school." I imagined how such times could be fun. Then I could do something on my own. Maybe I'd get a bicycle and ride back and forth to school by myself.

I thought about the photograph of Tara. Maybe that one had been taken during a difficult time when Aunt Tanja was always crying, forgetting to wash Tara's clothes, give her a handkerchief or wake her in the morning...

Mom was irritated with Dad, because he had made that crack about Uncle Tony. "Anton is not crazy!" she said. "And don't say those things when that child is around." I had to go to bed, and before I fell asleep, I kind of liked that they were coming: Uncle Tony who might be crazy and Aunt Tanja who was most definitely crazy and forgot things. Only Tara didn't appeal to me. I wished her mother would forget to bring *her* to Cape Cod.

2

Cape Cod is a long peninsula in the Atlantic Ocean. Our house is there, on the outskirts of a city called Truro, on the edge of the sand dunes. If you look through our kitchen window you only see dunes and, in the distance, almost at the ocean, a big, ramshackle house where no one has lived for a long time. No one wants to live there, supposedly because it is too far from the city or because the foundation is loose. But everyone knows there is another reason.

On a cold day in the fall, when the house was still empty, I went there with my friend David. David was the only kid my age who lived at the beach. All the other kids from school lived in Truro. I didn't have anyone to play with except him.

"I know a hole where we can get through," he said.

I was scared, because even standing outside you could hear a lot of tapping and ticking noises underneath the roof. David talked about how Goody Hallett, the witch who rides on the back of whales, had lived there.

"Don't be scared," he said. "Goody Hallett was swallowed by a whale. The whale hunters found her red shoes in the stomach of a sperm whale. She is dead now."

I was only eight then and still very superstitious. I asked myself whether the witch hadn't just left her shoes behind in the stomach of a sperm whale and escaped through the spout hole.

Afraid of being left alone, I also went inside, through the hole in the blue front door. We climbed underneath a carving of the tail of a mermaid with ugly warts and a hooked nose.

"Her name is Siren," said David, and he put his hand on the gigantic tail fin.

"How do you know that?"

"It says underneath." He pointed to some elegantly carved letters in the wood. I didn't look at them closely, though. I wanted to get through the hall to the dining room as quickly as possible. There was a tall door with dull glass and a gilded knob. It was ajar and creaked a little when David pushed it open.

In Goody Hallett's house, each day was like Christmas. The sturdy table in the dining room was set for at least thirteen people. There were menu cards with German Christmas designs and streamers hanging down from the ceiling. There was a tree with ornaments as big as melons. Withered branches decked with faded red ribbons hung on the wall. Grey wreathes, with acorns and walnut shells glued on, hung from the doors. Underneath the chairs was a wine red carpet, the same red as the napkins on the plates. I knew that the napkins were much redder than they looked. You could tell by the edges that the dust had turned them ashy pale. The backs were still deep red. The flowers in the small vases stood there, brown and frail, with their little heads bent down.

"Sit wherever you want," David whispered. I didn't sit down, because the chairs were much too high and covered with dust. I looked at the candlesticks. They were coated with congealed wax. Big drops of candle wax had also fallen on the rug.

"They didn't even blow out the candles when they left," I said, more to myself than to David. David stood on the other side of the room at the big windows looking out over the ocean.

"Anna, come here," he called. The sudden sound of his voice scared me. I rushed over so that he wouldn't call a second time.

"Look at this cigar," he said and pointed to a long, charred sausage that had kept the shape of a cigar.

"They left in a hurry. No one knows why or where to. It was all because of little Filip's disappearance."

I'd often heard that story about Filip at school. Filip was a toddler from Truro a long time ago. On a warm day, he'd disappeared from the beach. Some said they had seen him walk to this house. After that, he'd vanished without a trace.

"Goody Hallett turned Filip into stone," said David in a solemn voice. "Come with me."

He led me to a plaster statue on the floor against the wall. It was a stark naked, chubby boy with fat little fingers and arms stretched out slightly, as if he expected applause.

"Was this ever a real child?" I asked, reaching out my hand to touch it. David pushed my arm away roughly.

"Absolutely. My dad knew the baby. He had curly hair and looked just like this child."

"Isn't this an angel?" I asked while I looked at the two severed stumps that protruded from the child's shoulders. I could tell by the pieces of plaster on the floor that they had been wings.

"Of course not, stupid. It wasn't an angel. It was a normal boy just like all the boys in town. The witch turned him into stone. She turns anything she likes into stone. She can turn your legs into stone so you can't walk anymore. Or your arms if you touch something." He pointed at my arms. I was scared and wanted to go home.

"Have you seen this?" David asked, trying to distract me. He pointed at the presents underneath the Christmas tree. There were at least six or seven, all wrapped in colourful paper and different in size.

"Oh!" I said excitedly. "Should we open them, David?"

He shook his head. "Each time I come here, I want to open them. But my dad told me not to touch anything in this house. If we do, our hands will turn into stone."

I looked at my hands as though they weren't mine. The wind blew stronger now and the wood creaked upstairs. "Let's go," I said. As we left, I noticed that the mermaid on the blue door had more warts on her face than before.

Mom could tell I had been in the beach house by the dust on my coat. She started to beat my coat with the clothes brush, hard enough for me to feel the wooden handle.

"Don't go there, Anna. That's private property."

"Does Goody Hallett really exist?" I asked, crying because she was hurting me.

"No, witches don't exist. And certainly not Goody Hallett. People only tell those stories to scare each other." I knew she was lying. I went upstairs and played haunted house with my dollhouse.

"Tonight we'll ask Dad," I said to Smart Doll, who was angry because no one told her the truth.

That night, at the dinner table, I asked Dad to tell me everything, including the creepy parts.

"Did you know little Filip, Dad?"

"Which little Filip?"

"Little Filip who turned into stone because he touched something in Goody Hallett's house."

He smiled. "Do they still tell those stories at school?" He looked at Mom and said, "They told those in my time. And, of course, we were all terrified."

"Dad, why is it always Christmas at Goody Hallett's?"

"No one knows, sweetheart. Very rich people used to live there. One Christmas Eve, they all left. No one knows where they went."

"Why didn't they take the stone Filip?"

Dad looked at Mom. She nodded. "Might as well tell her the whole story now," she said while I shifted to the edge of my seat. Dad quickly put another bite of cabbage in his mouth, swallowed and took off his glasses.

"People mix together two different stories," he said. "One is a whaler's folktale. Witches don't exist, so little girls don't have to worry about them. The other one is about a little boy who went to play in the dunes one day in the fall, and then disappeared. It took a long time for the police to find any traces. But, in the end, the people who lived in the beach house became suspects. Then, the day before Christmas, I think in 1957, the child's body was found buried in the dunes."

"Was he still alive?" I asked, barely able to breathe.

"No. The police proved that the young son who lived in the beach house had killed the child."

I looked at my plate and felt a piece of cabbage rising slowly in my throat. "Why killed?" I mumbled.

"Oh, he was a strange boy. He molested little Filip and…"

Suddenly Mom clacked her tongue. She pushed her glass back and forth on the table top, looking at Dad.

"What does 'molested' mean?" I asked. I could feel something was wrong.

"It means to hurt," Mom said quickly, so that I knew she wasn't telling the whole truth.

While I lay in bed that night, I began to suspect that "molested" meant the same thing as "turned into stone." Goody Hallett now seemed terrifying and I swore I'd never enter her house again.

Throughout the next fall and winter, David kept begging me to go with him.

"You'll get four pieces of chalk if you come with me," he said.

I knew he didn't dare go alone, because I had told him Dad had said that the little boy really had turned into stone, and that Goody Hallett returns each year to celebrate Christmas.

David taunted, "You always know when she comes, because her voice sounds like a storm wind. 'She is the demon of screaming,' Thom Klika always says. She screams like a steamer when it storms. At night, you can see her coming across the ocean from afar. She rides on the back of a whale and her lantern hangs on the whale's tail. That's how she deceives the fishermen with her light. When a boat goes missing, it's her fault."

"But didn't you say she was swallowed by a whale?" I asked. He smiled mysteriously, but didn't answer. I was still young then and fell for everything he said. In the mean time, I got to know the beach house much better, because Uncle Tony and Aunt Tanja went to live there. Now I know witches don't exist. Even when people look like witches, it doesn't mean they are. Yet, I still don't feel entirely safe in that house. So Goody Hallett didn't live there, but maybe an angry old woman who locked children in her cellar, or handed out deadly poisonous candy, did. Something about that house still gives me that feeling, especially after Tara entrusted me with what happened to her between those walls.

3

It took a long time for Aunt Tanja to arrive. I waited in the dunes and watched people walk in the wind on the white beach. A woman wearing a knitted scarf walked with a man over the soft rolling dunes right up to the water. Once in a while the man stopped for something in the sand. He bent to pick it up and show her. They talked about it and she nodded. They walked back to the paved road again. After that, a man riding a horse trotted by. The horse was grey and covered with mud. A man with a child and a kite came. The man constantly straightened the little one's hat. There was a dog with shaggy hair that sniffed everything and made the seagulls angry. No one else was on the beach. I was bored. I hoped Aunt Tanja would come soon.

When Anton Myrold and his family arrived, I saw only Aunt Tanja. I watched her closely, trying to see what was crazy about her. I examined her purse and earrings. With each movement she made, the dainty green balls on her ear lobes softly clicked against each other. Is it possible to go insane hearing that noise all day?

She was beautiful. I wished she was my mother, because she was slim. My mother was fat, and I didn't like that then. Actually, Aunt Tanja was thin. She didn't have breasts. She was completely flat in front, like a boy. There was no bra strap on her shoulder. She drank coffee all day long and said "Not too much!" when Mom tried to fill her cup.

"It has all been just too difficult," she said in a voice that sounded like a violin. "That apartment is so small and Anton spoils that child to death. All I do is stupid work that drives me crazy. And the rent in Cleveland is so high. Every last cent disappears. My clothes are old and worn out. The doctor gave me tranquilizers and then told me I was taking too many. Those men don't know what they're doing. They think they know what's wrong with you. Meanwhile, you just pay the bills."

I wished she was crazier. She looked quite normal with her jeans and yellowish brown shoes and big rings on her fingers. Her finger nails were short and the skin around them was red and swollen. The fingers on her right hand were yellowish brown from nicotine. Uncle Tony immediately went off with Dad, so I couldn't tell by him either. They said they were going to buy a car and then going to a real estate office. I thought there was enough room for Aunt Tanja and her husband in our house. Maybe Tara could live somewhere else.

"Anton isn't like he used to be," Aunt Tanja said. "He is — how should I say — so indifferent, if you know what I mean."

Mom looked at her and then at me.

"Anna, why don't you show Tara your camp?" she asked. Only then did I see that Tara Myrold stood in front of me. She hardly resembled the child in the picture behind the cupboard in the garage. She no longer wore glasses, because she'd had an eye operation.

"She used to have a lazy eye, but now everything's fine," said her mother. She pointed at Tara as if she was talking about a TV announcer whom she had read about in a women's magazine. Tara stared out the window and didn't listen. Her hair was thin, but not as thin as in the picture. Her clothes were trendy and brand new. She wore a black ladies' watch with a second hand, and sandals identical to mine. Her most striking feature, I thought, was her long curly eyelashes. I had never seen anything like them: she had eyes like a horse, or a doll. At first, I thought they were creepy. Later, I thought they were beautiful. She didn't smell like her picture either. She smelled quite ordinary: a bit like chalk and soup, and of course like an airplane.

She was small. She only came up to my shoulders. That made her look younger. She looked like a mouse. Trying to be friendly, I led her outside to show her my camp behind the dunes. She didn't follow me and I realized then that she didn't care about my camp. I threw some stones on the metal roof of the garage and listened to the empty sound.

Dad and Uncle Tony came back a few hours later. They talked for a while by the car before they went inside.

"In the fall, especially in September and October, you'll be able to find something to do here if you're prepared to do seasonal work. During the cranberry harvest. Hard work, about fourteen hours a day, but it's not bad pay. I can ask the A.D. Makepeace Company. They always need workers."

I sat down on the wall next to the garage without a word.

"This box was left in the trunk," said Dad as he lifted a carton covered with brown tape.

"Careful with that," yelled Uncle Anton as he jumped forward. He quickly took the box from Dad and put it on the ground.

"Rather fragile," he said. He wore a T-shirt that said CLEVELAND INDIANS. "These are old singles that belonged to my mother. Great music from the fifties. I'll let you hear them sometime."

"Your — uh — mother?" said Dad doubtfully as he coughed. "I thought she — "

Uncle Tony nodded. "I never knew her. She died when I was two. But it's her collection. My dad wasn't attached to them. He couldn't stand me listening to them. But I loved that music so much." He knelt down by the box and began to pull off long pieces of tape. He yanked the flaps back and gleefully showed us the row of records. He pulled one out. It said FRANK SINATRA. I tried to read the rest, but he put it back. He looked at it tenderly, as if looking at a nest of newborn kittens.

"Can I hear them too?" I asked. He sat down next to me on the wall and pulled at one nostril. Without answering my question, he said, "Sometimes I let Tara listen. She loves them as much as I do. That child knows what's beautiful." He fished a pebble out of his Nike and tossed it behind him.

"Maybe we could consider that secondhand Buick," he said suddenly in Dad's direction. He pulled his ring finger until it cracked loudly.

"Can I hear them too?" I repeated impatiently.

He stood up, picked up the box with records and took them inside. I jumped up and sat down again.

"He doesn't listen to me," I said to Dad. He came up to me and took my hand.

"Come on," he said. And we went inside.

Tara never came to visit my camp when I was there. In the beginning, I waited for her because I hoped she'd want to play wife and make stone soup and sand bread while I went hunting. But she never came. She just stood on a dune and looked out over the ocean, "to see whales," said her mother. Sometimes, she went in the water, even if it was quite cold, always wearing her red T-shirt. Underneath it was an old-fashioned bathing suit that came down to her thighs. She crouched in the water and stayed there, shaking, for several minutes. When her mother came to get her, she wasn't angry. She didn't even say "You'll get pneumonia." She just gave her a towel and walked home without looking back.

Tara hadn't said very much to me until one particular morning, when she suddenly appeared. I was busy putting in new sticks on the windy side of my camp.

"Let's hope it doesn't rain today," she said. Her voice didn't scare me. It sounded like I had expected: husky and without a sawing sound. More like the voice of a woman in front of a microphone than that of a girl. I looked up. There was a clear blue sky. It hadn't rained for days and on TV they said it would take a while before we'd get any.

"It's not going to rain today," I said confidently as I planted my stick deeper.

"You don't know that," she said walking off. When I went home that afternoon, I asked Mom for my raincoat. For some reason I thought it might rain.

I knew she came into my camp to play at night, long after I had a bath and got into my pyjamas. She switched around all my things and added odd objects she'd found on the beach. She made a door where there was a window, and used the pot for cooking buffaloes as a bed for her doll.

That was later, when the Myrolds lived in the old beach

house. But for the first few weeks they lived with us and I had to share my bed with Tara. We'd go upstairs as if nothing was up. But as soon as we were in my room, she'd become annoying.

To start with, she insisted that I face the wall for several minutes while she got undressed. She'd stand behind the closet door and keep a towel around her the whole time.

"If you turn around, I'll scratch your eyes out," she said. Once she was finished, she let me get undressed. From my bed she boldly watched all my movements. I made sure I was finished and in bed next to her very quickly.

"Leave the light on," she said. At first I thought she was scared of the dark, but after a few days I understood that she wanted to look at the light bulb. She lay there for a while and looked into the bright light with her eyes wide open. She didn't even blink. I rolled onto my back and tried it too.

"It hurts!" I cried, squeezing my eyes shut. I could still see the bright yellow spot on my retina.

"Yes," she said without moving. She kept both hands clasped around the sheets like claws, until suddenly she turned her face with a little shriek and shut her eyes tightly.

After that the light could be turned off. In the dark she hissed that I had to lie on the floor.

"I can't sleep with someone lying next to me," she claimed.

"If I lie on the floor, I'll still be lying next to you," I tried.

"It's not the same," she said. "My stomach wobbles when you move around. It makes me have to go to the bathroom all night." I wasn't going to let this strange creature take over my bed. But she moved diagonally across the bed, her feet against my back and pushed so hard that I tumbled out. I thought she wanted to play and started to laugh, jumped on top of her and tried to push her to the side. She rolled back and forth. For a moment I thought I heard her laugh too, but I was wrong. I felt her search for my hand in the dark and then put her teeth in it. I screamed and landed my fist on her nose. We were both in a lot of pain, but because she didn't call out for her mother, I didn't want to call downstairs either.

"This is *my* bed," I said to myself, "and she's not going to throw me out." Tara curled up in one corner, I on the other side and that's how we fell asleep. Sometimes at night I woke up in pain because she kicked me in my stomach.

4

My parents often spoke about Tara Myrold.

"What's wrong with that child?" my dad said. "When I look at her, she immediately turns around. When I approach her, she tells me to go away. She doesn't answer when I ask her about school."

"She's just very shy," my mother responded. They continued to talk about Tara for a long time, but I left the kitchen.

"I continuously feel like saying 'Tara, look at me!' or 'Answer my question!' or 'Take your thumb out of your mouth!' Isn't she a little old to be sucking her thumb?" I heard Dad say. Mom mumbled something soothing. Dad continued his comments: "Tanja doesn't occupy herself enough with that child. Only Tony pays attention, almost too much, I'd say."

I went to my room. I was tired of hearing about her. Even when Tara herself was around, I always wandered off. Then one day, she burst out in anger on the beach. She yelled, "Anna, come here. Come and *play* with me. Your mother says so."

I saw Mom cut across the sand with her apron still on. By the time she got to my camp, she was red-faced and out of breath. She said, "Anna, play with your cousin! Don't be so self absorbed. Tara is your friend, isn't she?" Tara pouted with a very aggrieved expression on her face.

"Anna takes all my toys away from me," she said. Mom looked at me. "And if I get closer, she yells dirty words."

I think Mom knew Tara was lying, because she didn't scold me. She just said, "Oh, go on and play. I have to get back to cooking," and she walked away across the dunes. I sulked for a while. At first, I didn't want to play with her at all, but was persuaded by the great-coloured shovels she had. Tara let me dig with one of them, the smallest one with a wooden handle and an orange shaft. It was still wrapped in plastic.

"Just got it from Dad this morning," she said, seeing my surprise. I knelt down and started digging into the sand. I wanted to dig a brook, but she insisted on a mountain with a pit next to it. When I helped her build the mountain, however, she started the brook. In the end, when I helped her with the brook, she demanded a brook that ran away from the ocean instead of toward it. I gave up and turned to dig by myself. Suddenly she stopped digging and glared at me.

"Give me back my shovel!" she said, but I pretended not to hear her. She waited a bit, then filled her shovel with sand and leaned toward me. I thought she was about to fill in my brook, but instead, she threw the shovelful of sand right in my face. I roared. My eyes and mouth were full of sand. It tasted awful. It stung my eyes and grated between my teeth. I left quickly for home but when Mom asked what had happened, I told her I had fallen.

That's how it was for the first few weeks of Tara's stay in Cape Cod. She slept in my bed, but was usually allowed to stay up much later than me. Each time she laid down beside me late at night, she pushed me to the edge of the bed with all her strength. Sometimes Uncle Tony came and tucked her in. They'd whisper to each other for a while, he with the deep voice of a man and she with the deep voice of a woman. I put the pillow over my head and tried to sleep without dreaming of her lying next to me.

In the middle of the night, I woke up because she moaned in her sleep. She sounded as though someone was strangling her. I waited anxiously for her breathing to stop altogether. But she tossed and turned for a while, then fell quiet and continued to breathe normally.

Even during the day she was very mean. She always wanted to play with me when I didn't want to, but Mom made me. I played with her because no one else my age lived in my neighbourhood, and because she got so many great toys from her dad. The ends of her hair started to curl more and more, but on the top of her head it was still very thin and fragile. Her eyelashes kept getting longer. Sometimes I thought her eyes were beautiful, but usually they scared me.

When we played together, we usually didn't talk much, because as soon as we did, we fought. I always thought she'd started it but I tried to be nice anyway. Sometimes I'd start the day planning to cooperate with everything she wanted to do so we could finally become friends. But then I'd get to my camp and find that all the branches had been taken down off the roof and dragged into the ocean. Or all five of my dolls had mud in their eyes and their hair. Then I'd be angry, so angry I'd almost explode.

To take revenge, I cut her jacket that she left in my camp the day before, to pieces. She just folded the pieces, put them in her bag and took them to her mother. "Mom, look what Anna did now."

Her mother talked to my mother. My parents were furious.

"This isn't like you, Anna. You've never done anything like this before. What's gotten into you?" I cried for a very long time that day.

At school, Tara was a problem. Everyone took my side and no one could stand her. She always wanted the exact opposite of what was happening, something else, to have it her way. Even our teacher, Ms. Abbelese, didn't like her. Now and then she'd say "Tara, what's the matter with you?" and, if her patience had run out, "Tara, you're unbearable. Go outside immediately."

She wasn't bad or anything, but she seemed to go against the grain on purpose so that everyone avoided her. The strangest thing, I thought, was that she never cried. Not even when everyone chased her away and called her names. It was as if she somehow expected it. The teachers asked, "Is this how they do things in Cleveland?"

Sometimes you could see her get frightened, because someone who didn't know her was being friendly. Normally, she didn't talk to anyone, especially not to me. In the mornings, she'd only say "Give me your homework!" and then she'd copy all of my work while we waited for the bell. A few times I failed my homework. "Not done on your own," it said in red.

David was one of the first boys at school who got to know her.

"Are you in Anna's class?" he asked Tara. "That's impossible. You look a lot younger. You look the same age as my little sister."

I knew he shouldn't have said that. I took a few steps back, in case Tara got angry. Tara stood there with her hands on her hips. She leaned on one leg, and gave him a defiant look. "Are you the David from next door? Anna's told me about you. She thinks you're a wimp. Apparently you're afraid of seawitches.' David looked at me with eyes like knives. I turned away.

"You always get bad marks too," she said to make it even worse. I don't know why I had told her all that. I forgot to mention that he was my best friend, I guess. David dug his heels into the sand, spat on the ground and said, "At school they say your lucky number is 1. That's crackers. No one in their right mind chooses 1 as their lucky number. Maybe 11, or 7. You're as crazy as your mother!"

Tara ran toward him and elbowed him between the ribs. After that she quickly disappeared between the pine trees. David looked at me and spat again.

"If you play with that freak, stay away from me. I'd rather play with my sister." I blinked my eyes and looked for words.

"Big mouth!" he hissed and walked away cursing. I felt as though my feet were stuck in the sand and couldn't go after him.

5

In the beginning, we took Uncle Tony, Aunt Tanja and Tara everywhere. They had to get to know the stores, the bank, the library and the school in Truro. When we walked through the streets, I could feel people looking at us. We were a strange bunch. I always walked way ahead of Mom and Dad, who held hands or had their arms intertwined. I remembered how, when I was a little girl, I always walked in between them, my little hands tightly held in theirs. They'd let me jump and sometimes fly...I couldn't get enough of it.

"That's enough," Dad had finally said. "Anna has to walk on her own now. Dad's arm is tired, and so is Mom's."

"Yes, mine too," Mom had confirmed when I'd looked at her pleadingly. At that moment I decided I was too old to hold hands. Since then, I preferred to walk in front of them, so I didn't have to listen to their boring conversations about new washers and sick cousins. If I walked ahead, I got to decide which street we took, and was the first to see anything exciting going on.

I thought Tara would want to walk up front with me. But I soon realized that the Myrolds walked differently. Aunt Tanja and Uncle Tony didn't walk next to each other, but one behind the other. Sometimes she walked in front, sometimes he did. Tara always held her dad's hand. She carried on the most childish conversation with him I could imagine.

"Truro is at the ocean, right, Dad? Finally we live by the ocean!" At the traffic lights, she called shamelessly, "Red! Look, Dad, we have to stop. Red means 'stop.' Everyone stops. Then, when it's green, we can go on."

I was so embarrassed to belong to this group that I walked at least half a block ahead of everyone.

"Anna, we're going in here," Mom called back to me. She waved at me from the entrance to a gigantic apartment building.

I traced my steps back and followed her through the glass door. FOR RENT, it said.

"There are a few places for rent. Anton is going to find out about them." Uncle Tony talked to the woman at the counter for a few minutes. Tara stood right next to him while Aunt Tanja waited on a chair. The clerk showed them pictures of houses and apartment buildings, and once in a while Uncle Tony wrote something down.

Suddenly, something seemed to grab Tara's attention. She began to talk quickly and squeezed her dad's hand while shaking her head. He looked at her and then at the clerk. She pulled his shirt, and he nodded. I watched them without paying attention to the other people in the room. I watched him massage her shoulders and bend toward her when he spoke to her. Although he was tall and thin, he was also handsome. His T-shirt hung loosely over his jeans in front. He snapped his fingers like a cowboy and wore a bandanna around his neck. For a moment I wished I had a dad like Uncle Tony.

A short while later, the three of them reported that there was an apartment for rent in the Fisherman's Building, right underneath the First Bank. It was large, but quite expensive and didn't have a garden.

"There are a few other apartments that aren't worth seeing, because they have only one bedroom. That's just as bad as our apartment in Cleveland. And...this..." he said, and quickly searched through the papers in his hands. He pulled out a small scrap of white paper with his handwriting on it.

"She told me that the beach house not far from you is finally up for rent. Somebody bought the place and is planning to auction off the household items on Thursday. And the rent will be relatively low, although I don't know why."

In a flash, I saw Mom and Dad look at each other. "Goody Hallett," I thought immediately. "One night Tara will turn into stone and stand next to little Filip forever. Aunt Tanja and Uncle Tony will have to celebrate Christmas all year long and eat dust off the greenish red plates."

"I've heard the house is beautiful, Anton," said Dad as he

put his hand on Uncle Tony's shoulder. "It's gigantic. It will be quite different from before. But of course, you don't have to use all the rooms."

Uncle Anton nodded, and Tara was quiet again.

"I wonder why the rent is so low," Aunt Tanja mused from her chair.

"Stories," Mom said promptly. "Weird stories about witches and children turned into stone. At one time, a child was killed by a resident of the house. When the news came out, the whole family left the house within hours. Because they left behind all of their furniture, it has always seemed a little creepy. The whole thing happened almost thirty years ago, but the fishermen with their superstitions keep scaring the kids. People around here are crazy."

"I'm not scared," Tara said suddenly. Dad smiled at her as he stroked her hair. She quickly took a step back. Dad's hand hung in the air for a moment. Then, with a dry cough, he pulled his arm back.

"Of course you're not scared," he said to regain composure. "The beach house is the most beautiful house in Truro."

After the auction, I was especially worried about the presents.

"They didn't sell the presents that were under the Christmas tree," I told Mom excitedly. She smiled. She had dinner waiting for Dad and me. My favourite pizza was warming in the oven.

"That Anton doesn't know what he's doing," Dad muttered. He threw his jacket over the chair and started to untie his shoes. "He bought a few things, but he could've gotten much more. All in all, he bought two beds and two mattresses. The beds went for no more than twenty dollars and another ten for the mattresses. That idiot. He lives in a house with ten bedrooms and buys two beds! He can't even have someone stay over."

He grabbed a piece of bread, and Mom handed a piece to me.

"Then he bid on a kitchen table and four chairs. Cupboards galore. If I'm not mistaken, he bought five of them. He wanted more, but the bid went too high. It made sense, because they were antiques. Those things were incredibly expensive. Robert claims the high bid on the son's paintings came from the family. Everything went by telephone. All the junk is left behind for Anton and Tanja. Only the furniture and linen were sold off. And, of course, all the china and pewter and so on. Everything of value is gone. But they have enough pieces of carpet, old lamps, racks, boxes, baskets, books and pots to last a lifetime."

"And the presents!" I yelled eagerly.

"Yes, and they're stuck with that enormous Christmas tree and all those decorations, paper junk and broken windows. They'll have a lot to clean up."

"Dad, do you think I could have one of the presents from underneath the Christmas tree?" Mom gave me another piece of bread and said, "Anna, everything belongs to your aunt and uncle now. What they do with it is their business. It'll only be junk anyway."

I didn't believe in junk. Junk didn't exist. Everything in Goody Hallett's house was special and fascinating and beautiful, so it couldn't be junk. At the most it could be ugly, or broken, or a stupid screw driver with a pair of pincers. Certainly it was all very delicate and valuable. Perhaps the big parcel was a wooden box with a key. If you opened it, a ballerina would pop out and begin to dance to soft organ music coming from underneath her pointed feet. And the small parcel had to be a box of stamps or some books about adventures on islands full of dinosaurs. The smallest one probably contained a metal box with a window showing the date and day of the month. Or a key chain with a locket that held a tiny photograph. Or a fancy pen in which a miniature coach with horses rides up and down while you write. Or a ring with a golden stone.

"But are you allowed to touch them?" I thought in sudden panic. What if the hand that opened the music box turns into stone? Or your eyes when you read the adventures? Or the finger with the golden ring?

"Maybe it's better Tara keeps all the presents for herself after all," I said in a deep voice, and Mom nodded approvingly.

"Will Tara live in the beach house instead of here from now on?" I asked. "Mmm," said Mom, and Dad repeated for the third time that day how strange he thought it was that Anton didn't want to stay with them one hour longer than necessary.

"The house is a disaster," he said, "and still they want to move in. I don't know what's gotten into those people."

I could only think about how happy I was to have my bed all to myself again.

That same day, the Myrolds came to get all their belongings. Uncle Tony was arranging his records in a box when Tara began to whine about toys.

"When I live by myself, I'll have nothing to play with anymore. Everything belongs to Anna."

Uncle Tony talked to her in a soothing voice. "I'll buy you everything new, darling. You know that, don't you?"

"I don't want anything new. I want this!" she yelled and pointed at my puzzles and model ships. She angrily started to stamp her feet. Mom threw a disturbed look at her sister, but Aunt Tanja just kept packing her summer stuff.

"Tara darling, just ask Anna to lend you something instead of carrying on like that," Uncle Tony said very patiently.

Tara's face relaxed. "I want my Smart Doll," she demanded.

"Anna?" Uncle Tony said. He looked at me for a long time. Mom nodded, and I knew I no longer had any choice.

"She can take her," I said. "I don't play with her anymore anyway." When Tara walked out of the house with my doll upside down under her arm, I felt robbed. At the same time, I felt she was powerful, and that she knew how to get whatever she wanted.

I understood that, from now on, it would be impossible to avoid Tara. Now that she no longer lived with me, I'd want to know what she was doing. I had to see the house, the attic and the basement, and I wanted to be there when she opened the presents. I wanted to help with the cleaning and put the books on the shelves, the baskets in the racks and the pots in the cupboards. I'd find stone fingers and feet everywhere, but that was exciting. I couldn't let this chance go by. Tara had to become my friend.

When I went to visit her the following morning, she was drawing on the ground with huge pieces of chalk. She had already put some strange scratches on the wall of the house — they looked like waves with angular points — there were more on the shutters. Here and there, she drew an animal over them, a fish or a bird, and something with four legs that I didn't recognize.

"I have chalk," she called before I could say anything. "I draw with it." I went to stand right next to her and looked at the thin hair on her head as she was bent over. She looked up.

"If you leave right away, you'll get a piece," she said. She stood right in front of me like an angry dwarf, and I didn't quite know what she'd said. I wanted a piece of chalk, but I didn't want to leave at all. I had come for the presents, and didn't want to leave before I'd seen what was inside them.

"What was in the parcels?" I asked quickly. She stood up and handed me a piece of chalk.

"Here," she said. "Take it." I took the chalk and looked at it. I looked at it for a long time, because what I held in my hand was the strangest thing I'd ever seen. It was a while before I recognized it. But then I knew what it was, and it gave me the chills: it was a stone hand. The small hand of a toddler. It looked as though it was still alive and moving.

"Little Filip," I uttered. "This is little Filip's hand."

"Oh," Tara said, "that was just an old statue. Mom didn't like it, so Dad smashed it up for me to write with. Now I can draw the ocean everywhere, and later I'll add words. But now leave me alone. Go and draw on your own house."

I threw Filip's hand on the ground and went home through the dunes. I wished from my gut that Tara had never, ever come.

6

I sat on some driftwood and cried for a while. In retrospect, I could've gone to David or Dad, but it didn't occur to me. When I had no more tears left, I wiped my face and went back. She was busy writing letters, an *s*, an *e* and an *a*. Beside her on the ground stood a glass of greenish lemonade. Her dad always gave her lemonade, as much as she wanted. We only had juice.

"If you open the presents, your hands will turn into stone," I said quickly, but she didn't turn around. I came closer and said, "Goody Hallett turns everything into stone. If you lie, she turns your mouth into stone. If you take something that's not yours, your hands turn into stone. If you kick people who share your bed, your foot turns into stone." I knew that wasn't quite what David had said, but I wanted her to be really scared. "If Goody Hallett spits in your lemonade, and you drink it, your intestines turn into stone. So you better watch it when you drink." I tried to think of even worse, but she just kept on writing. I knew Tara had the ability to close her ears in the same way other people close their eyes. She drew pictures of fish, wrote an *f*, after that an *i* and then an *s* and an *h*, and didn't notice me. She only seemed to notice me when I approached with heavy steps and nudged her with my knee. It seemed as though plugs had shot out of her ears.

"What do you want?" she asked.

"I said your intestines will turn into stone if Goody Hallett spits in your lemonade." She looked at her glass, slightly surprised, and then pointed at her T-shirt.

"Not when you wear red. When you wear red, nothing can happen to you," she said solemnly. "Or when you ride a red bike."

"A red bike?" I asked with some misgivings. Would her dad give her a red bike? She pointed at something in the bushes. I went to look and saw a racer. The frame was deep red and coloured ribbons hung from the handle bars. It was the greatest bike I'd ever seen.

"From your dad?" I asked needlessly.

"Yes," she said. "If you come with me to look for shells, I'll let you ride it." I nodded eagerly.

We went to the beach together, each carrying a bucket. Tara didn't know anything about beaches — she only knew about alleys and basements — so I led the way.

"This is bad timing," I said. "It's high tide. We'll have to come back later to look for shells. There's nothing now." But she was persistent.

"Search," she said abruptly.

We searched for a long time. Not all shells were good enough for Tara: they couldn't be broken or cracked. Perfect shells were few. That's why we had to wait for low tide.

"She doesn't have a clue about the ocean," I muttered with my face to the sand. We walked farther and farther away from the beach house. Our buckets filled up slowly with unremarkable shells and bits of ocean debris.

A fisherman was standing in the water wearing high green waders. "Let's see what he has," I called, pointing at him. Even though we sped up, it took a while to get to his buckets filled with bait and loot. From a distance, we saw a large fish lying next to the bucket. Tara started to jog toward it.

"A shark," she called back at me. "A baby shark. He just caught this one, it's still moving." I approached cautiously, because I was afraid of sharks. The animal was as long as my leg and had big gill clefts on both sides of its head. Tara got very close, watched the tiny eyes and stroked the slowly moving tail.

"What a sweetie," she said.

"Sharks are awful," I explained. It was clear she didn't know anything about fish. "Sharks eat people and other fish. They're crazy about the smell of blood and tear their victim to pieces." I stayed away from the vicious beast as far as possible, because the more I talked about it, the more anxious I got. It could bite her hand off.

"It's still so young," she said, unperturbed. "Just because it eats people doesn't mean it can't be sweet." I repeated her words in my head a few times, but doubted them. Can an animal be bloodthirsty and at the same time be sweet? She interrupted my thoughts. "He's as sweet as my dad," she said, and I thought of the red bike, the presents underneath the Christmas tree and the broken sculpture.

After we walked back along the whole stretch of the beach, Tara convinced me to do one more thing before I was allowed on her bike: build a sand castle with her. I remembered the fight a few weeks before, but decided not to think about it. From now on, Tara was my friend, and with friends you build sand castles.

I'd made tons of sand castles before, so for me it was no big deal. I could build castles with underground tunnels and bars for the doors and windows made from twigs. My castles even had battlements — or something similar — and trees in their gardens. Today, a moat with actual water in it might be a bit too much work. After all, I still wanted to go for a bike ride and check out Goody Hallett's presents.

Tara started on her castle without much deliberation. She just packed some sand into a pile and walked around it.

"First you have to mark the outline," I said, drawing a circle in the sand with a shovel. "That's how you figure out the size." She continued to throw around loose sand. "And you have to use wet sand. Wipe away the dry sand, then we can build."

"Can't you just throw ocean water on top?" she interrupted.

Didn't she know that if you use water, the whole thing would turn into a mud bath? We needed cold sand that had been damp for days. I wondered whether it was worth it to have Tara as a friend. She didn't have a clue about the ocean and the beach, and maybe she'd never let me in her house. Maybe Goody Hallett's Christmas presents had already been put away or thrown out, and I'd never see them.

"Do you think the presents contain little arms and legs out of stone?" I asked as I watched how she tried to control the loose sand. But she wasn't listening. I don't think she even knew I was there. She walked to the ocean with a bucket, came back with water and poured it over her castle. Her pile washed away, and she looked at the mud bath.

I heard her mumble, "More water," and she went back to the shore. She walked back and forth with her feet in the water, and looked at everything that moved underneath her. Suddenly she jerked. She put down her bucket and threw her head back. She didn't make any noise, but I could tell that something was wrong. She stopped with the palm of her hand pressed against her mouth. I jumped up and ran toward her.

"If I bite my hand hard, the bleeding hurts less," she said. Her teeth left deep marks in her skin. I looked down at her foot and saw the water around it turning light pink.

"Glass!" I shouted. I'd stepped in glass dozens of times, but I'd never seen that much blood. I'd cried every time until my mother came to get me and put an ice pack on it. But Tara didn't even sob. Instead, she bit down on her hand.

"Go to your mother," I said slightly panicking. "She should put an ice pack on it." Tara waved her other hand.

"It'll pass. I'll bite my hand until I don't feel my foot." She walked to the dry sand and sat for a while. I stood beside her. The sand in the wound stopped the bleeding. Her hands rested beside her. "If someone ever hurts you, make sure the teeth in your hand hurt even more. Then you won't feel the other."

I dug my toes into the sand, first my left foot, then my right. Pain is pain, I thought, whether it's your hand or your foot. What difference does it make? We sat like that for quite a long time. She didn't do anything to keep the wound clean. She refused my handkerchief. Neither did she go to her mother.

"Leave me alone now," she said suddenly. I looked at her in surprise. She hadn't shown me what was in the parcels yet.

"And the bike?" I asked.

She got up, took her bucket and headed for home.

"You won't get the bike," she said abruptly. "You didn't keep your promise. You didn't build a sand castle." I braced myself with anger. She turned around when she realized that I was no longer following, and called, "There were no stone arms and fingers in the Christmas presents at all. You'll never guess what was in them."

So she had opened them. Her hands hadn't turned into stone when she undid the knots and tore the packing paper. I went after her, but she started to run with a limp and disappeared through the door with the ugly mermaid. I walked around the house while trying to look inside to see whether the contents of the parcels might be on the table, or somewhere on the floor. But I only saw boxes and paper and junk. Everything was the same as yesterday. Except, there were no more presents underneath the tree. Most of the curtains were drawn. The red bike lay in the bushes, but I didn't dare take it. Mom and Dad would probably think that letting the air out of the tires was as mean as cutting a jacket to pieces.

There were traces of dark red sand on the narrow porch. There was a half empty glass of yellowish green lemonade on one of the tiles. It had gone flat and the ice cubes had melted. Beside it was Tara's drawing of the word FISH. I knelt down by the glass and gathered spit in my mouth. Then I spat into the glass and sped home.

7

On stormy days, Aunt Tanja and Tara would come to visit us.

"I can't stand that hammering and rumbling in the attic," said Aunt Tanja. The green balls on her earrings made a soft ticking noise each time she moved her head. She took a carton of juice out of our fridge and poured herself a glass.

"Me too," called Tara.

"First ask your aunt," said her mother. Mom nodded and poured me some too. Sand blew against the window and a window upstairs banged. That was the window with the broken lock. I recognized the noise. Mom asked me to go up and shut it properly.

Tara followed me up the stairs. She pressed her schoolbag under her arm. It probably contained a difficult assignment or something. I knew I'd have to help her again.

"I brought them with me," she whispered. I pretended not to hear her because of the strong wind.

"I brought them with me," she repeated a bit louder and quickly looked around the room.

"The parcels," I thought immediately, but didn't move. I sat on my bed and stayed there until she slowly opened the buckles of her bag. She was so slow that it scared me.

"Little stone hands," I kept thinking. "Broken little hands and feet and heads, a little face with a cracked cheek. A stomach in half. An ear that fell off." I could tell by the noise of the ocean that the storm had picked up. It was a hurricane, the hurricane that would bring back Goody Hallett — "the demon of scream- ing," according to Thom Klika. I dug my nails into the bedspread and listened to the wind. The clicking of Tara's buckles scared me so much that I almost peed my pants. I faced away from the window, because I could feel the ugly mermaid, Siren, looking at us. Mechanically, I ran my fingers through my ponytail. The day before, I'd gone swimming, and the saltwater had made my hair hard.

"I don't want to see them," I said with difficulty. Tara directed her eyes at me in surprise and closed her bag again. That was too bad, because I did want to see them. Then again, I didn't. Not in my room. Not where I had to sleep alone all night with the storm above my head.

"Anna!" Mom called from downstairs. I jumped up and shot down the steps. Tara was right behind me.

"Your popcorn is ready," she said when I was halfway down the stairs. "You've been whining about it all afternoon."

The kitchen smelled like popcorn. It was the smell of fairs and winter evenings. Aunt Tanja shook some salt over it, lazily, without getting up from the table.

"She had to live by the ocean," she said as if she hadn't heard us come in. "And if Tara wants something, she gets it. Her dad takes care of that. She wanted to live by the ocean to get to know the fish, he said. Fish! That's why I have to live a secluded life. It drives me crazy." I stopped chewing when she said that. Did she mean really crazy?

"I can't raise that child with that man around," she continued while watching Tara. "He lets her do whatever she wants." She filled her mouth with popcorn.

"He lets her do whatever she wants," Tara repeated in the same tone.

"When I tell her to go to bed, he lets her come back downstairs and watch TV with him for hours."

"...for hours," echoed Tara. She said her mother's words at the same time. She said each word the same way as her mother did, in the same tone and with the same breathing spaces. Like a poem they had rattled off together thousands of times: "When I tell her there won't be dessert, if she doesn't finish her vegetables, he gives her his dessert and finishes her vegetables." Aunt Tanja gave her daughter a disturbed look. She paused for a moment.

"In the stores, she gets everything she wants," they continued in unison.

"She wears the most beautiful clothes!" said Aunt Tanja quickly. But Tara was fast and said the words with her.

"Tara Myrold, for God's sake, shut your mouth," shrieked Aunt Tanja suddenly. A little drop of spit from her mouth made a loop and landed in the bowl of popcorn. Mom soothed her.

"Calm down, Tanja," she said. I looked at the popcorn in disgust and tried to estimate where the spit had landed.

"When Tara was a baby, Anton never paid any attention to her. I had to do everything on my own. He always took off if she cried, or was wet, or hungry. But now it's always Tara, Tara, Tara. I don't understand it."

Mom pushed the popcorn over to Tara. "Here, have some more," she said softly. Tara grabbed a handful. I wasn't sure whether she'd taken the drop of spit as well.

"What about you, Anna? You wanted popcorn so badly, and now you act as though it's poison." I shrugged my shoulders. First, I wanted to wait and see what would happen to Tara. Mom dug her hand down into the bowl and put the white fluffs in her mouth one by one. There was a strange noise between her teeth.

"Anton doesn't pay attention to me anymore. I went to a tanning salon and lost weight, but nothing helps. He acts as if —" Mom grabbed her by the shoulder.

She pushed the popcorn into my hands and opened the door. "You go and play in your room," she stressed.

They're being secretive again. The sisters have to talk about things no one is allowed to hear. Like a puppet, I went in my room. The window with the broken lock had blown open again. I hurried to it and threw out the contents of the bowl for the seagulls. Then I shut the window and wedged it.

"Now we're safe," I thought as I watched the foaming crests of the ocean in the distance. "Do you really get everything you want in the store?" I asked Tara.

"My dad tells me I'm his doll," she said. It thundered. How strange to be someone's doll. I wished I had a dad who bought everything for me and finished my vegetables. A dad like Uncle Tony, who kissed me all the time and said "Sweetie," and gave me presents every day. Maybe he'd call me doll too. And at Christmas time there'd be a doll for me underneath the tree.

"Mom says the same thing every day. I can rhyme it off," she said a bit later. Then she kept silent for a while.

"Where's the popcorn?" she asked as she pointed at the empty bowl.

"I threw it," I said awkwardly. "It was dangerous. It had spit in it and spit turns you into stone. But we're safe now. The window's stuck shut." I smiled.

"So, do you want to see them then?" she asked, and I nodded. She opened the buckles as I got closer on my knees. She took some bright objects out of her bag and lined them up on the carpet.

"This is what was in them. I opened the presents and thought they were things you can wear, T-shirts or undershirts or something. But that's not it. Can you guess what it is if I unfold it?' She held a small roll of bright red cloth in front of my nose. I pulled back and shrugged my shoulders.

"Hocus pocus," she called as she unrolled the thing. She held up a bright flag.

"Now do you know what it is?" she asked.

"Of course I know," I said calmly. "It's a windbag."

"Exactly," she exclaimed. "When I opened it, I didn't know what a windbag was. In our apartment in Cleveland, we didn't have a balcony. So we didn't have a windbag to hang outside either. But Dad explained what it was. He had one too, when he was little." I couldn't listen to her for sheer disappointment.

"A windbag!" I couldn't believe that Goody Hallett had windbags underneath her Christmas tree. Windbags are kind of fun, but they aren't really of any use. Goody Hallett could at least have given an ornament, a hair pin, or a brooch with a gold-coloured pin, or a book with secret sayings. But a windbag! Nice but useless! They're bright, and you hang them outside in a tree, or on a pole so that the wind can play with them. All you can do is look at them and see where the wind comes from. What got into Goody Hallett to give something like that?

"Were all the presents windbags?" I asked.

"There were six of them, and a book. The book is at home. I want to hang the windbags on the balcony off my room. Dad says I can have them all."

"But what happened to the big presents? Weren't there big presents as well?"

"These are them. They were in big boxes with a lot of newspaper." She folded the reddish yellow windbag again. I wished she'd give me one, because the colours were very beautiful.

"If it storms, the wind will break them," I said to scare her.

"The red ones won't break," she said convinced. "Red means 'Stop.' It means you're protected, from the wind as well. If you wear red, you're safe. That's why red is my favourite colour." She pointed at her red sweater importantly. Then she looked at the window being shaken by the wind, but it was firmly wedged shut.

"Are you scared of Goody Hallett too?" she asked solemnly. I thought I'd fall through the floor. Had she seen me watch? Had she seen the Siren's face in the window too? Had she recognized Goody's singing?

"Witches don't exist," I said firmly. She nodded and smiled. Things were calming down a bit outside.

"Tara! We're going home!" her mother called from downstairs. "Your dad's waiting for you!" She was startled and jumped up.

"Here," Tara said, holding up the windbags. "You can choose." I pointed at one with a lot of orange.

"Orange is quite nice," she said. And I heard her think, "But not that safe." I watched her until she got downstairs. Through the window, I saw mother and daughter walk across the dunes. Their hair stood back horizontally, and Aunt Tanja stooped with her hands on her chest. She walked in front and didn't look back.

Tara dawdled. She stopped to pick something up or to re-arrange her coat. But Aunt Tanja didn't turn around or call her. It looked as though they were each walking through the storm by themself.

8

Tara wasn't doing well in school. Ms. Abbelese couldn't stand it when Tara was off in another world.

"Are you deaf?" she'd say, and you could tell by her fast-moving fingers that she was about to start yelling. But Tara kept her eyes absentmindedly on the blackboard. Mechanically, she'd take a couple of candies out of the bag on her lap, and didn't sense that the whole class was looking at her.

"Is she ever strange," the boy beside me whispered.

"Her mother's crazy," I answered just as quietly, "and it's now getting her too."

"Tara Myrold. Stop eating candy when I talk to you," Ms. Abbelese repeated with a false calm in her voice.

Tara swallowed her spit and concentrated on the burning feeling on the roof of her mouth. We could all taste the sweet syrup on our own tongues by watching her. She looked at Ms. Abbelese obligingly and nodded.

"That's better," said Ms. Abbelese. "And now listen to what I say..."

Slowly she repeated that everyone had to cooperate. That she had to do her math. That she had to listen to the teacher. While she talked, Tara crammed one candy after the other in her mouth until it was jampacked.

I happened to be in the beach house when Ms. Abbelese came to talk to Aunt Tanja about Tara. I saw the poor woman's surprise upon seeing the yellowish brown Christmas tree in the corner and the broken plaster angel on the floor. She hesitated at the sight of the blue sparkling streamer that hung from the ceiling. She half smiled and pushed pieces of wrapping paper aside with her foot.

"Big house," she said to Aunt Tanja, who laughed out loud.

"Big houses drive me crazy," she said in a shrill voice. She moved to the gigantic gold-framed mirror, brushed through her hair and pulled at her green earrings that hung almost to her shoulders. "We left Cleveland because we didn't have enough room. The doctor told me I needed rest and space. Tara wanted to live by the ocean, so we came to live by the ocean. Away from everything. I have a degree and am wasting my life here."

This visibly startled Ms. Abbelese, and Tara giggled from behind the couch. "I had to buy a dryer. I can't dry laundry in the wind, because everything smells like fish. And the thought of gardening here is just absurd." Aunt Tanja fell silent, and Ms. Abbelese didn't say anything either.

"Have a seat," said Aunt Tanja, pointing at a dusty wooden chair. She herself sprawled out on the couch. Ms. Abbelese sat down.

"I'm here because of Tara," she said carefully.

"Tara, go upstairs and play with Anna for a while," said Aunt Tanja firmly. I got up and shook the chalk out of my pants. When I saw that Tara hadn't budged, I stayed behind the door.

"She doesn't listen to me," said Aunt Tanja in a plaintive voice that I recognized. "That's because of her father. He lets her do anything she wants. When I tell her to go to bed, he lets her come back downstairs and watch TV with him for hours. When I tell her there won't be dessert, if she doesn't finish her vegetables, he gives her his dessert and finishes her vegetables. In the stores, she gets anything she wants. She wears the most beautiful clothes. When Tara was a baby, Anton never paid any attention to her. I had to do everything on my own, and he always took off if she cried, or was wet, or hungry. She had fuzzy hair and wore glasses. She was the ugliest child on the block. But now that she's been operated on and her hair is a bit thicker, you can't tear him away from her. Tara's a saint. Together, they gang up on me. They'd rather be cozy here with just the two of them and put me in a home for frustrated mothers. I should be grateful I'm still allowed to stay overnight. But all that sand in the house just drives me crazy. And that wind! It blows around the house like a screaming siren." The word "siren" startled me, but I kept quiet.

Ms. Abbelese kept rubbing her hands back and forth as she listened. Tara plucked wool from the couch and concentrated on the bits of fluff. I knew she didn't hear anything they said. Aunt Tanja flung one leg over the arm of the chair and continued: "She's such a hothead. She gets angry about nothing. She brings me these silly drawings of fish and bottles and says, 'Look, Mom, just look. Don't you see it. Look closely.' When I tell her that I only see fish and bottles and the ocean, she gets so angry she pulls the hair out of her head. And she doesn't have that much."

I looked at her thin hair and long eyelashes from behind the door. It felt strange to listen to this long grown ups' conversation. It didn't bother Tara, but it bothered me. "Spoiled," "dad," "solution," "discipline," "approach " and "obedience" came up so often I began to get bored. I listened more carefully again when I heard my name.

"I think Tara and Anna should be together as much as possible. Anna's a good example. She always listens and does her work. Maybe they can sit next to each other in class from now on." When Ms. Abbelese said that, I panicked — I didn't want to be next to Tara in class. Nobody wanted to sit next to her. That's why she'd been sitting by herself at the back all along. I jumped up and walked toward them.

"I don't want to sit next to Tara," I said without thinking.

"Anna," Ms. Abbelese exclaimed indignantly, "Were you listening? I thought you were gone." Tara jumped up and grabbed my arm. She pulled me upstairs to her room.

"You have to sit next to me in class," she nagged. "You're a good example." I didn't answer and went to the balcony. From there, you could see the boats. You could see everything that washed up, pieces of driftwood and plastic bags. I felt Tara move beside me.

"Do you think you can see Europe from here?" she asked.

"Europe?" I repeated in surprise.

"Yes, Europe. I saw on the map that there's only an ocean between us and Europe. It seems they wear wooden shoes there and that everybody knows everybody. They have small villages everywhere and churches with steeples and weathercocks, and even the cars are small. People live in very old houses made out of brick instead of wood. There are trains full of kids. They all wear uniforms for school, and if you wave at them, they wave back. There are horses in the streets pulling coaches that you can ride around all day if you want. There are flowers everywhere as well."

I bent over the railing to see if I could see land. Then I sat down on the wooden floor with my face to the sun.

"How come you haven't put up the windbags yet?" I asked. I'd seen them rolled up in a corner of her room, beside Smart Doll who lay face down on the floor without legs.

"You can have them all. I don't want them," she said.

"Really?" I asked distrustfully.

"Except for the red one. That one I'll hang inside. But you can have all the other ones. I don't want them on my balcony. There are too many colours. They'd attract too much attention, people might look in to see what they are." Her hair was flat in the wind, and she looked bald. "I don't want people to look in."

I went inside and unrolled my new treasures one by one. They were breathtakingly beautiful with their bright colours. One of them even had purple stripes.

"I want to keep this one," she said and pointed to the one with red stripes. I didn't mind. I imagined how beautifully the rest would hang on our porch at home. I'd show Dad exactly where I wanted them, and we'd watch them all summer long.

"Did you know the wolf didn't eat Little Red Riding Hood, because her mother put a red cap on her. Red means: don't touch me."

"The wolf did eat Little Red Riding Hood," I said as softly as possible, because I was afraid she'd scold me.

"No, he didn't, you stupid twit. You don't know anything about fairy tales. Dad told me himself." She strode over to a shelf and picked up a book. It said *Fairy Tales*. Fiercely, she started to leaf through the book, then stopped when she heard someone in the hallway. The door swung open and Uncle Tony walked in.

"Tara darling, what are you doing?" he asked. He didn't say anything to me. Tara didn't move, the book still in her hands. She didn't seem to hear him.

"We're reading a book," I interrupted. He sat down beside me on the bed. He leaned his elbows on his knees and brushed his hand through his hair. He sighed a few times, looked at Tara and then at me. Tara didn't move.

"I just talked to that teacher of yours," he said heavily. "You have to do your homework together tonight."

"I don't have my books," I thought quickly. Uncle Tony went to stand behind Tara and started to massage her shoulders.

"Tara's going to sleep at your house tonight," he said with his head back. "It's better if she's not here. It doesn't do either of us any good." He left making a sobbing sound. A bit later, we heard loud music blaring from the other bedroom.

"Frank Sinatra," Tara said, without explanation.

Tara was still clenching the book of fairy tales under her arm when we left the beach house. My hands were full carrying the windbags. The red bike was still in the bushes, in the same spot as a few weeks before.

"You can't bike on sand," she said.

I thought about the bike for the rest of the evening. I also thought about Uncle Tony, and about his music. But Mom and Dad didn't find it strange that Tara was staying at our house. After we finished our homework, we had to go to bed. There were two pink pillows again, just like when Tara had stayed with us before.

"Face to the wall and don't look," she commanded. I stood against the wall with my hands in fists. I hated all this fuss. I didn't want it to start all over again. I didn't want to stand there and face the wall in my own room.

"Can't you act normal?" I asked.

"If you look at things you're not allowed to see, your eyes will turn into stone, remember?" she said. "If you talk about things you're not allowed to see, your mouth will turn into stone.

~ 42 ~

Do you want a mouth of stone?" I didn't say anything and touched my lips with my index finger.

When she was ready, I was allowed to get changed. She lay down in the position I recognized from before: knees pulled up against her chest with her arms folded in between. She crawled underneath the blankets until she looked like a little heap of rags.

"Dad promised to hang the windbags tomorrow," I said to break the silence. She didn't move.

"We still have to look at the Little Red Riding Hood book," I said, because I was sure the wolf had eaten Little Red Riding Hood. She didn't answer and remained motionless. She didn't even move when I noisily started to leaf through pages, until I found the fairy tale. In elegant letters it said LITTLE RED RIDING HOOD. The next page had a drawing of Little Red Riding Hood, but it had been cut. Her mouth had been sliced out with small scissors. The next page showed Little Red Riding Hood talking with her mother. "Would you take this basket to your grandmother?" it read underneath the picture. The girl's mouth had been coloured shut with a black felt pen. Yet a page further, there was Little Red Riding Hood picking flowers. The lower half of her face had disappeared.

Tara threw the blankets back and pulled the book out of my hands. Quickly she turned the pages.

"Here!" she said and she showed the very last page where Grandmother and Little Red Riding Hood were hugging. "See, she wasn't eaten. She's still alive."

"She's still alive, but she *was* eaten. The hunter saved her," I persisted. She lifted the book and whirled it across the room as far as she could. It fell like a dead bird and smashed onto the floor. She pulled the blankets over her head and said, "I can't believe how stupid you are. You just don't get it." For a moment, she was quiet and it looked as though she had stopped breathing.

"If Little Red Riding Hood can escape from the stomach of an animal, then so can Goody Hallett. But maybe with a bit of luck, the bottles will come out again too."

The thought that Goody Hallett might not be dead alarmed

me for a second. Then I fell asleep. Now and then, Tara's tossing startled me. Sometimes she called out strange things without waking up. Then I looked out the window to where the dancing windbags would be tomorrow, until I fell asleep again.

9

The next morning, Mom started to complain about a toothache. Immediately, I thought of the popcorn with the spit in it.

"Your mouth is bewitched, Mom," I said, dead serious. I knew Aunt Tanja had told her secrets. "If you tell secrets, your mouth turns into stone. That's because you swallowed spit."

Mom smiled at me and brushed my hair back. "Where did you get all that nonsense?" she asked. I began to tie my shoe laces. Mom looked at Tara who sat behind a bowl of Corn Flakes on the other side of the room. She bent toward me and whispered, "Anna, don't believe what Tara tells you. She's a little strange. If she tells you something, come and ask me whether it's true, okay?"

I went into the living room to get my bag, and she walked with me.

"Tara's bewitched as well," I said quickly. "She thinks sharks are sweet. And she's afraid people will come and look at her windbags. She even bites her hand when she's in pain. And she never wants to get changed when I'm there."

"Oh really?" said Mom, but nothing more.

"She cut out Little Red Riding Hood's mouth," I continued. "And she builds castles with dry sand. I really think she's bewitched." Mom gave me a long look when I said that. Then I had to go to school.

When I got home that night, the windbags were already hanging. It was a wonderful sight, the colourful windbags on the beams of the porch, all of them sloping in the wind.

"Take a picture of them, Mom!" I yelled excitedly. She smiled and remained seated. I went into the backyard to see them from that side. The house had gotten much nicer. A small airplane flew over very low, and the grass sloped in the same direction as the windbags. Behind me I heard the ocean.

"I'll get Tara to show her," I yelled excitedly. Before I could leave, Mom grabbed my hand.

"Tara shouldn't be here too often," she said. "Once a week is more than enough. I called Ms. Abbelese about it and she agrees." I nodded. I could phone her later and tell her she should look out the window. She could probably see the bags from the attic of the beach house.

"And your tooth?" I asked. She waved her hand. The phone rang and she went into the hall to answer it. It had to be Aunt Tanja, because Mom only grumbled to Aunt Tanja.

"Who was it?" I asked when she came back inside.

"Tanja wants to know if Tara can sleep here tonight. She says it's an emergency."

"Why an emergency?"

"Oh, she's too tired to take care of Tara. It'll be better tomorrow."

Dad came home late that night. We were in bed already, but not asleep yet. Tara turned on the light as soon as she heard his voice in the hallway. She pulled herself up right in front of the light on the night table and watched the door. Her thin hair was bathed in a halo of light, but I couldn't see her eyes.

"Will he come in?" she asked.

"Of course not," I answered lazily.

"Does he hurt you when he comes in?" she asked right after that.

"He gives me a kiss. Sometimes he tickles me so hard, I almost die laughing, or he rubs my back if I'm itchy or can't fall asleep. But that doesn't hurt." I reached for the light switch, because the light bothered my eyes.

"Don't!" she yelled. "Leave it on. He'll scare us too much if he comes in, and then before we know it he'll lie down next to us." I thought that was ridiculous. I put the pillow over my head and tried to go to sleep.

"I wish I was Goody Hallett, inside the stomach of a whale,

where no one could find me," she said, more to herself than to me. I heard Mom talking in a high-pitched voice in the room next to us. I could only make out "Tara" and "not good for Anna."

"Ugh!" I moaned from underneath the pillow. "How gross. Do you have any idea what the stomach of a whale looks like? Whales eat balls, rope, pieces of net and boards and bottles and…"

"They eat bottles too?" Tara asked in her mother's voice. "That's horrible!"

"Not more horrible than a board."

"Much more horrible than a board," she said emphatically. "I'll probably dream about it." I sat up straight. She stared with eyes open wide into the light again. Now I heard Dad's soothing voice.

"Having wonderful dreams and waking up in the middle of the night is great," I said. "Then you can go back to sleep, because it isn't morning yet." She punched me as though I'd said something wrong. I moaned. Why was it so quiet in the next room?

"Do you like waking up in the middle of the night!? You could wake up and find someone in the room who wants to hurt you. I hate waking up. Besides, waking up in Goody Hallett's house is really creepy. Maybe she visits during the night."

"Who knows whether Goody Hallett ever really lived in the beach house. Mom says they're just stories."

In the room next to us, Mom was telling the story from that morning. I could feel it. Her words zoomed through my head like bees: "Anna, don't believe what Tara tells you. She's a little strange. If she tells you something, come and ask me whether it's true." Suddenly, Tara's face was very close to mine. I could feel the warmth of her breath.

"Of course Goody Hallett lived in the beach house. She had to have a house right by the ocean, because she didn't have legs." I looked at her questioningly. I'd never heard of a Goody without legs. She nodded violently.

"Goody Hallett only had a fish tail, like the siren on the door." My stomach turned slightly.

"But what about the red shoes?" I asked in a tiny voice.

"What do I know," she grumbled. "In any case, I get scared when I wake up at night." I sat up straight. She made me uneasy. I didn't want to be uneasy, and not scared either, not until I'd asked Mom.

"Anything scares you," I mumbled to encourage myself. Immediately, I felt a shooting pain in my arm.

When I got into bed the next evening, I found a folder underneath her pink pillow. Now that she was far away at the beach house, I had the chance to go through her papers quietly.

The folder was almost empty. It had a few meaningless drawings that didn't tell me anything. Then there was a crumpled letter that I smoothed out before reading it. It had a strange message: SOS EUROPE. COME TO CAPE COD, TO THE BEACH HOUSE (IF I SAY ANYTHING, MY MOUTH WILL TURN INTO STONE).

There was also a page from a book, a book about a shipwreck or something like it. One of the passages was underlined. I read through it quickly, but it didn't interest me. I also read the second passage that was underlined: "He filled one fifth of the bottle with sand, so that it would stand up straight in the water. Then he tightened the cork. And now, let's hope the water won't get in, he thought. He swirled the bottle into the ocean, and watched the floating object until it disappeared from sight."

I quickly closed the folder when I thought I heard Tara's voice underneath my window.

10

Tara's school work wasn't getting any better.

"She's not mature enough for the material," Ms. Abbelese had said to Aunt Tanja. "There's a strange contradiction within that child: she's so worldly, and yet can't follow the class. I think it would be better if she repeated her grade. Maybe she needs some more time to get adjusted."

I knew, secretly, that Mom was happy Tara would no longer be in my class. Then she wouldn't be able to copy my homework or borrow my books. Uncle Tony protested vehemently when he heard about it. But Ms. Abbelese persisted. Tara didn't pay attention to their bickering on the phone. All summer long, she was consumed with her collection of capped bottles. I didn't ask any questions, when I handed her the empty bottles from our kitchen. There were dozens of white, brown and green glass bottles in her room.

Sometimes she'd play with me, but not very often. Every morning Mom would say, "Why don't you go and see David. You used to be best friends. Maybe next year, he'll sit beside you again in school." But David was never there. If he wasn't visiting his grandmother in New York, he was skateboarding on the concrete behind the A.D. Makepeace factory with his friends.

"Can't you see I'm busy," he snapped. I even tried to stand on a skateboard, but fell on my tailbone when David pushed me. I slunk away to the library and borrowed a ton of books. From that moment on, I knew what I'd do: I'd read myself through the summer holidays. I could see Tara cross the dunes from my reading corner, but not once did I make the effort to go outside.

Aunt Tanja was getting more beautiful by the day. She was now responsible for sales at the candle factory and didn't visit much anymore. Besides, following Dad's suggestion, she was planning to clean the entire beach house, so that she could rent out the rooms to tourists next summer.

"You could get filthy rich," Dad had said. "People from outside Cape Cod are not scared off by haunted houses like the foolish fishermen around here." At the end of the summer, Aunt Tanja came to ask if we wanted to help work on the house. It had to be rearranged and cleaned, swept and painted. I was glad I could help. I loved all those boxes, drawers, corners and rooms in which you could nose around for hours and get the feeling you were in a crowded market where you could buy anything.

Sometimes Tara helped, but not usually. I was allowed to work on my own, when Mom and Aunt Tanja had to go to Truro for business. That was the most fun. I'd stand on the balcony and look out over the ocean as if I were the countess of the house.

"I see Europe." Via the balcony, I went into Aunt Tanja's bedroom and put on her clothes. I put makeup on and went back to the balcony.

On the beach down below, I saw Uncle Tony and Tara sitting on a towel. Tara wore her high-cut bathing suit with a red T-shirt over it. Uncle Tony wore swimming trunks with wide stripes. He talked to her gently, and smiled now and then. The sun felt strange on my makeup. It felt as though the red of my lips would start to drip in the heat.

Uncle Tony got up and walked toward the water. He waded in the shallow water, then slid his whole body into it and started to swim without splashing. His head got smaller and smaller, until it was a little cone.

"A cone head," I thought. "Look here, I'm the countess of cone heads." Then I thought, "Uncle Tony's going too far into the ocean. He'll never come back, because the sharks will devour him." I went to wash off the makeup in the kitchen. I folded the clothes as well as I could and put them back where I'd found them. Then I went to the closet in the hall and tried on all of Aunt Tanja's high-heeled shoes. There was one pair of red ones, completely covered in dust.

"Maybe they're from the stomach of a whale," I thought out

loud. I sat down on the couch by the door and tried them on. The next moment, the door swung open, and Uncle Tony strode in. His wet hair was much darker than usual, and his swimming trunks stuck to his thighs. He didn't see me because his eyes hadn't yet adjusted to the light indoors. He went straight upstairs, to the bathroom. Quickly I undid the straps of the red shoes and tiptoed to the closet barefoot.

I walked quietly so that Uncle Tony wouldn't hear me go up the stairs. I went upstairs to see who he was talking to. The bathroom door was open, and I heard him talk in a high-pitched, almost singing voice. He stood there bent over the sink. There was nobody else to talk to. There was a big picture of Tara above the toilet, but that wasn't unusual: the house was full of pictures of her.

"First rinse off that saltwater," he said. "And then a lot of aftershave. Man, you always smell so nice! Oh, that's all natural. Now a comb. Where did that rotten comb go." I started to blush — or did the makeup irritate my skin? — and hid behind a pillar in the hall.

"Real man!" I heard him moan a bit later. He turned on the small recorder that was always by the sink and started to sing along: "Start spreading the news — I'm leaving today — I wanna wake up in a city — that never sleeps — New York — New York." I tiptoed down the stairs, grabbed my shoes in the hall and left the house.

A few weeks later, Uncle Tony started to work for the A.D. Makepeace Company. His hands were always purple from the cranberries, and his back was bothering him a bit. Tara and I were back at school, but we didn't sit together on the bus. I always sat with David, and at night he'd come home with me to do our homework together. Then we played together. He taught me how to skateboard and I showed him all my books. We watched a lot of TV and things were just like they were before Tara moved to Cape Cod. Mom was content.

One afternoon in November, a thick fog moved in over Truro. Through the windows of the classroom, we watched it get dark.

It was quite normal for the time of year. Once we were on the schoolbus, the driver made an unusual announcement over the microphone: "After you get off, walk home in groups. Stay on the road and don't go into the dunes or the bushes. Watch out for cars, but stay on the pavement." The boys began to whistle and the girls rolled their eyes.

"Fog's great," David groaned, and the boys howled even louder. Tara, David and I had to get off at the Highland light-house.

"Tara, make sure you stay with us," I said when the bus left. I immediately knew I shouldn't have said that. She looked at me furiously and snapped, "I'm not a baby." Her breath trailed out of her mouth. She straightened her shoulders and started walking. We tried to keep up with her, but when we saw her walk into the sand, we stopped.

"You'll get lost!" David yelled, and it sounded more like a tease than a warning.

"You'd rather be alone, wouldn't you!" she yelled sharply. "So you can neck!" I felt my face go red.

"That witch!" David hissed. He followed her, and I scrambled behind with my hands in my pockets. The sand broke under our feet. I knew exactly where I was and tried to keep track of Tara through the fog.

"Where's she going so fast?" David panted.

"This is the way home. She knows the beach," I said.

A short while later, she'd completely disappeared in the fog. "David, we have to stay together. Let's not be like Tara. Tara's a little crazy," I said, wondering where the beach grass was that should've been on the right side of our path. The little pine tree with the pile of rocks wasn't there either. I tried to match his steps.

"Do you still know where we are?" David asked.

"You?"

"I think this is the big dip, but I'm not sure." David stopped and whistled between his front teeth.

"It's all that witch's fault," he said. "That kid lives in Goody Hallett's house. That's why so many things go wrong. We're going in the wrong direction." He tried to orient himself. "Here's a pine tree. Let's sit under it until the fog lifts a bit." He crouched underneath the branches and sat on his bag. "You're not afraid, are you?"

"No," I lied. "We can't be far from home." David motioned at me to sit down, then looked over his shoulder to where he'd heard a little noise. He winked, and bent near to me.

"You have to be careful with that Tara," he sniffed. "Make sure you don't leave a piece of toenail within her reach. Make sure you don't leave a single hair in her room. Witches do horrible things to other people. If Goody helps her, she can make you sick from a distance."

"What do you mean, from a distance?" I asked. My voice sounded smaller than usual.

"They'll melt a piece of wax and put your hair or your nail in it. Then they'll model a figure that looks like you. If they put a needle in it, you'll be in horrible pain. If they chop off its wax head, you'll die." He spoke in a solemn voice. He looked at me from the corner of his eye. One eye was bigger than the other.

"I don't believe in witches," I said. screwing up my courage. He got out a pack of cigarettes, and matches.

"You smoke?" I asked.

"Goody Hallett smoked a pipe," he said without answering my question. "Watch out for women who smoke pipes. And watch out for women who wear red shoes!" He coughed as he lit the cigarette.

"Is it true that Goody Hallett had a fish tail instead of legs?" I asked.

"Of course. Goody was a mermaid."

"But what about the red shoes?"

"Those red shoes were just to confuse people. Nobody knew she didn't have legs, because she always wore a long dress. Only the count of the beach house suspected it. He invited her over for a glass of wine. Next, he flooded the entire room. When Goody came in, she pulled up her hem, so it wouldn't get wet. Right away, the count saw her tail. She married him, because he'd seen it."

"How do you know all that?" I asked with a catch in my voice.

"Thom Klika, the rainbow man, who lives beside the Cranberry. You know, the one with the store full of little rainbows."

I nodded.

"He told me a lot more. Do you want to hear it?" I breathed into my hands to warm them up and said nothing.

"Thom Klika says that Goody Hallett turned little Filip into stone. He claims that the child's spirit still wanders around. Especially when it's stormy or foggy, you can see him. He wanders through the dunes bare naked, crying out 'Mom! Mom!'" David imitated the wailing voice of a child. It sounded as if the noise came from behind us instead of from his mouth. I pulled my scarf around my head.

"I don't want to stay here, David," I said quickly. "I'm going home." I got up and waited for him to come along. I listened to every sound. After about twenty feet, I could make out the beach grass. Then the pine tree with the pile of rocks appeared.

"Do you remember Thanksgiving in Truro?" David rattled on. "Tara was completely covered in cranberry juice. Her hands were purple from the cranberries. It looked as though she'd fallen in a bloodbath." I started to walk faster, because I recognized the path. Then I saw the outlines of my house.

"We're here!" I yelled at David. Tears rolled out of my eyes as I stormed into the kitchen.

That whole winter, I didn't play with Tara once. Sometimes I'd bump into her at school, and notice each time that she'd grown a bit. Yet, she still only came up to my shoulders. I didn't look at her for very long, although I felt her batting her long eyelashes at me. I didn't see Aunt Tanja and Uncle Tony much either.

"Tanja's house is a big mess again," said Mom. "Not much will come of those plans to rent out rooms next summer."

David told me all the creepy stories he'd ever read. I got used to them, and wasn't scared anymore. I started to make up stories myself, and when I told him, he'd look at me pale as death.

"Awesome, Anna! What a fantastic creepy story! You should

write it down and make it into a book. Then we can make it into a film. You can be the witch and I'll be the spirit!" We'd act out our film, and in the evening we'd watch creepy videos. I never told him that I often woke up screaming in the night and slept with the light on.

In the spring, we'd make up stories about gravestones and storm winds. As summer got closer, goblins and poltergeists crept into our stories. In each story people died, and after a while they'd haunt the world of the living. Strange things would happen at night, and ordinary things during the day. Night was a time to sneak around and whisper, to hide and keep secrets.

Tara didn't know anything about our stories, and we liked it that way. It was our private world, and she didn't have to be part of it. We still didn't know that Tara lived what we made up.

11

Not long after that, something horrible happened. I was walking in the bushes covered with soft pink blossoms and squabbling larks. I was busy putting small insects into jars and had just caught a very strange, large beast. It was scary, but not enough to stop me from putting my jar over it and shoving the lid under it. I gawked at it in horror, and the beast looked at me with big angry eyes.

I didn't hear anything odd around me, but I could feel something was going on. I got up and stretched my legs. I tried to see as far as possible out across the dunes toward the ocean.

A bit farther, I saw Tara walking, faster than usual, away from her house, directly to mine. A trail of footprints followed her in the sand. Her eyes looked strange, like two big fireballs in her face. I knew she'd seen something horrible. Was it Goody Hallett? Was it little Filip with his hands of stone? Was it a shark that ate bottles? Was it the man in her room? Was it Little Red Riding Hood without a mouth? I didn't know and didn't have to know. No matter what had happened to her, Tara was a witch.

I kept on with my insect search, and when I couldn't find any more that I didn't already have, I took my five jars home. On the way, I stopped and examined an odd venus shell and a dried-up starfish.

I knew there'd be something going on with Tara, but didn't really care. When I entered the kitchen, Mom was writing something down. Dad was reading it over her shoulder. Tara stared in front of her, and Uncle Tony lay spread out on the couch with both his hand over his face. There were glasses of sherry out and Mom's face was wet and red. I joined Uncle Tony on the couch. He pulled in his legs a bit. He looked at me, and I looked back purposely, because he was picking his nose. I wanted him to take his finger out of his nose immediately, but his thoughts were far away. He didn't even seem to notice me looking at him.

"Aunt Tanja's dead," someone said.

"Yes, this time she's dead," someone else said. I thought to myself, "That's impossible! She's not even old yet! Maybe crazy people die young." Mom kept blowing her nose, and because I didn't know what else to do, I looked up names of insects in my *Book of Insects for Children*. When I finished, I took a stick of rhubarb from the fridge. I washed it, dipped it in sugar and took a bite. It tasted terribly sour, so I put some more sugar on it. As I sucked on the stick, I started to regret that I no longer had an aunt. It didn't occur to me that Tara no longer had a mother. Later on, Mom explained to me that Aunt Tanja had committed suicide. She swallowed a whole bunch of pills, and then just went to sleep. She didn't wake up, because pills are poisonous if you take too many. Tara thought she was still asleep, but when she took hold of her mother's hand, it seemed like the hand of a doll.

Later, I'd often dream about that. I'd dream I entered my parents' bedroom. Mom was asleep and looked pale, I touched her and she was completely cold. I'd wake up in the middle of the night and wouldn't be able to move out of fear. Sometimes I couldn't even shut my eyes, because they were paralyzed. Then I'd think: am I ever glad I'm not Tara.

"Why did Aunt Tanja want to be dead?" I asked.

"She was terribly depressed," Mom said. "That means you suddenly don't feel well, and you think nobody loves you. Everything is too much and you're in a bad mood."

"Oh, then I know what a depression is," I said. "Tara has one every day."

"I don't mean that," Mom said. She didn't add what she did mean. A bit later, I heard her say to Dad: "It would drive me crazy too — such a big house with no furniture and full of junk."

Two days after the funeral, I overheard Uncle Tony tell Dad that Aunt Tanja had often said she wanted to be dead. He walked beside Dad with his head between his shoulders just like a vulture. As soon as Dad wasn't watching, he'd start picking his nose. I tried not to watch, but watched anyway. He didn't stop when he noticed I was staring at him.

"She swallowed pills before, that time in Cleveland. I found her in time and they pumped her stomach. After that, she went to the institution in Chardon. The doctors there said she had to get out of the city, go to a quiet place, be with people who knew her. That's when I wrote you that letter."

I kicked stones and pretended not to listen. I squatted, picked something up and looked at it closely. This was the strangest story I'd ever heard. Why had Tara never told me anything about that? If my mother did something like that, I'd tell everybody.

But Tara didn't say anything. After her mother's death, she didn't come to school anymore and didn't sleep over with me. I'd see her wandering through the dunes in the morning while I was waiting for the bus. Sometimes she'd pulled her sweater over her head and walk along the beach like a blind person. I'd call her name, but she wouldn't hear me. She'd run up and down the beach, until she'd trip over a rock or a piece of rope. Then she'd pull down her sweater, look at her knee and limp home.

When I'd come home after school, she'd be lying in a dip in the sand, or running like mad through the bushes with bare legs. Her calves and shins would be covered in scratches, and from a distance I could see she was bleeding. After a while, she'd walk to the beach and stand in the saltwater. She'd go to places where the sandy beach turns into mud, and her legs would be grey when she came out.

For a long time I hardly talked to her. School was busy with tidying up the classroom, exchanging books and dreaming about holidays. I searched like crazy for a few lost books that had to be returned to the library. On top of that, I was looking for a present to give to the principal of our school. I didn't have any time at all to think about Tara.

On the first day of the holidays, I went outside and almost fell over her body. She was stretched out on one of the steps in front of our house, but she disappeared like lightning when she saw I wasn't at school. I followed to play with her. I wanted to walk through the empty rooms on the top floor of the beach house, or have a contest with her. But I couldn't get near her.

I followed her footsteps in the loose sand, but other steps confused me. Sometimes I could see her in the distance. She walked up to a bunch of seagulls with her arms extended. The birds took off screaming and started to circle around her. She threw rocks at driftwood in the water, yelled incomprehensible things at sailboats, hacked jellyfish to pieces with her shoe, broke knives, trampled sea urchins and tore apart starfish.

In the evenings, she'd stay up late watching TV. Dad mentioned that sometimes she still went to the beach afterward, and I was jealous, because I knew that, at night during high tide, you could see raccoons searching for shells.

The first time she spoke to me again, she said, "I'm going to ride the beach trolley." There was no beach trolley, not here and not for miles around. But at some point she'd said that every beach should have a beach trolley, otherwise it wasn't a real beach. The trolley had to have an open roof, so you could see all the passengers wave at the passersby.

Then she walked away, and sat and stared off into the dunes. From a distance, she looked like a little old woman, squatting with her thin hands between her thin legs. It was as if she might fall over at any second, or make shrill noises.

I went over to her, and when I bent down to sit beside her, she didn't move away. She took something round and sparkling out of her pocket, as if to show me.

"What is it?" I asked at least ten times. In the end, she held out her hand and let me see it. It was a gold ring.

"Dad gave it to me," she said. "It belonged to Mom. Look, it's engraved." I looked at it with squinting eyes. $1 + 1 = 1$, it said.

"That's wrong!" I exclaimed. "That's the wrong equation."

I realized crazy people are not very good at math.

"It belonged to Mom, but now it's mine. Dad told me to wait until my fingers are big enough." I let the thin object roll between my fingers, slid it on my thumb and wished I had a gold ring too.

"If you wear a ring, it means you're married to your dad," I said with a scornful smile. She jerked her head toward the ocean, and pressed her lips together. I pulled her arm and said, "Then you have to do things like sleep in the same bed. And then you'll get pregnant." She jumped up and pulled my hair really hard. I screamed. She ran off.

I thought there'd be another long period of silence, but I didn't care. The skin on my head, where she'd pulled, was completely red, and I sat quietly by the front door in the sun healing the pain. It was boiling hot. The crows behind our house walked around in the beach grass with their bills open. The seagulls spoke in long *rrr*'s and *aaa*'s, because it was summer. Little red spiders swarmed on the concrete. They walked around in circles. I squished them one by one with my finger and made little red blotches while I waited for time to pass.

Suddenly, I realized I was killing the poor things. For sure there'd be panic in the spider world now, and maybe somewhere a spider child cried, because I'd just crushed her mother.

"If you look at people from an airplane, they look just like little spiders," Tara's voice resonated right next to me. She'd read my mind, and the bump on my head started to glow immediately.

"Maybe someone's looking at us now, just like we're looking at the spiders," she continued. "Maybe Goody Hallett is so gigantic that we don't even notice her. Maybe that dune over there is her foot, and that one the other foot." She pointed at the slopes in the sand. "In a bit, Goody Hallett will stick out her finger and crush us because she's bored. Then she'll look at us and say, 'Such a cute little red blotch!'" I glanced at Tara while wiping the red off my finger onto my sweater.

"Do you believe Goody Hallett exists?" I asked directly. I knew everything had changed since Aunt Tanja's death. Her long eyelashes flapped up and down with each blink, and she made a strange, squeaky little noise.

"I don't believe in Goody Hallett anymore," she said. "I used to, but not anymore. That's why I'm not scared of her now either. Now I'm only scared of real things. Of people who die. Or of people who hurt you."

I rubbed the bump on my head.

"You hurt me," I said gruffly.

"Of course I hurt you. You're my friend!" she said. I could smell the sun on the concrete. I could also smell the water and the salt in the sand.

"You can smell everything much better, when it's warm," I said. But she wasn't listening. She was concentrating on crushing little spiders.

12

Again, Mom made me play with Tara every day, because Aunt Tanja had died.

"Be nice and do what I tell you. Tara's very sad and she needs a friend!" she said, before I went to the beach. Whether it was called for or not, Mom invited "the poor thing" over for dinner, to stay overnight or to go to Truro with us. David completely embarrassed me, when he laughed loudly with me as I dropped by. Luckily, he turned fourteen that year, and his dad made him work in a restaurant across the city. I hardly ever saw him, and if I did, he hardly said anything to me.

Although Tara told me she was my friend, she could still be really mean. Sometimes I thought, I can understand that her mother wanted to die. To have to live with a daughter like that would be Hell.

One day, after she'd just emptied my bag of chips without my knowledge, I was so angry that I said, "Gee, I hate you. Can't blame your mother for wanting to be dead. You drove her crazy." I'd often said really mean things to her, and usually she'd respond with something mean, or hit me on the head with her bag. But this time, she reacted completely differently.

Her big eyes filled with tears, she started to shake and a deep, long sound, like the growl of a young bear, came out of her throat. At first, I didn't quite realize what was happening, but then I saw she was crying, from deep down. I realized she'd never cried in my presence before. And actually, I felt kind of satisfied to see her sit on that bench, with her face all wet and her eyelashes stuck together, because this was exactly what she deserved for a change.

"Didn't drive her crazy," was all she could say. And again: "Didn't drive her crazy. Didn't drive her crazy." She sounded like a broken record. I walked away, so I wouldn't have to hear it anymore.

Since the day she'd cried with me, she followed me everywhere. She asked for help with her summer project and made dates to watch TV together. Sometimes, she talked about her mother for hours, and that seemed to provide relief.

"Did you ever notice that Tony, Tara and Tanja all start with a *t?*" she'd ask. "That's because we belong together. We're one family."

Then, for a while, it seemed as though Aunt Tanja had never existed. We played outside or inside, depending on the weather. We built fewer and fewer camps and sand castles — they were childish — but discovered new games for the summer: we juggled balls against the bluish grey walls of the beach house, or played bingo with Mom. Uncle Tony let us draw a hopscotch with chalk on his porch, and he took pictures of us. One Sunday, he took at least thirty pictures of Tara, and then left. Tara didn't seem to notice even for a second.

On rainy days, we sang songs in my room, or stencilled beautiful pictures on paper, wooden boxes and pieces of fabric. With a small knife, we cut out elegant flowers from thin stencil paper, and then we dipped our thick, round brushes into paint. We used very little, otherwise it blotched and the pastel tone got lost in a glare. We made birds, little houses and violet, light pink and sky-blue wreathes.

"Watch it, stupid! You're messing up my work," I'd yell and get away with it. She didn't get angry when I jeered at her. She'd flap her eyelashes and look down. I was rarely able to get her angry, but I was able to hurt her tremendously.

After I'd lashed out at her, she would sit in the hammock on the porch for a while. I'd join her and start whistling our songs. It would take some time before she'd sing along, but it usually worked. She'd calm down completely when I told her about the ocean, about anemones and seaweed, corals and sand banks.

She wanted to know everything about the ocean. She asked

questions I couldn't answer myself, and told me things I'd never heard before. After a while, I discovered she got them from a few books she'd borrowed from the library, but especially from that one book Goody Hallett gave her, the seventh present underneath the Christmas tree. It was a book about the ocean, with chapters about starfish, crabs, pilot fish, whales and plankton. Because of her independent study that summer, she knew more about the things in and around the beach than I did, even thought I'd lived there my whole life.

We searched the beach for shells from her book. On many a warm morning, we'd go snorkelling in the shallow water, she with her new snorkel, and me with my old one. Although the water was muddy, we still found the strangest treasures.

My arms and legs grew fast that summer. I went swimming with my shirt on, and with the approaching new school year, Mom bought me a bikini. Tara hardly grew at all. At school they called her "Tara Tot," or "Tot with the little red doll's clothes." They never said it when she was there though, because her mother was dead.

In the first few weeks of the new school year, I often noticed Ms. Abbelese talking to Tara during breaks. I didn't know what the conversations were about, and Tara didn't give anything away either. I suspect they were about Aunt Tanja, and what would happen with the Myrolds. It was clear Tara had difficulties concentrating in class, but the teachers were more understanding than they'd been before.

David no longer made any efforts to keep up our friendship. He hung out with boys his own age, and always sat in the back of the bus. There they let loose, whistling at girls and smoking cigarettes until the driver kicked them off.

"A womanizer!" Tara called him. She told me she saw him in the dunes with Laura from her class, and that same day with another girl, whom she didn't know. I never found out the truth. I do know David and his friends made a sport out of throwing rocks at young seagulls. Sometimes, they'd hit one of the birds in flight, and then they'd howl and curse so loud you could hear them in Truro.

13

Some time later, the pilot whales beached on Cape Cod. The event got on the front page of every newspaper, and suddenly it became so hectic that I almost forgot Aunt Tanja had ever existed.

I sat on the slope of a large dune and scratched a scab off my kneecap. The scab was hard, and underneath, yellow pus had hardened at the edges. Slowly, I picked at it, so it wouldn't hurt.

I'd been sitting there like that for a while, and when I looked up, I saw a lot of strange black shapes lying on the beach. At first, I thought they were overturned rowboats, but since no one was around that was impossible. The ocean made its usual sounds and spread its usual briny smell.

I got up to see better and climbed up the dune a bit. The objects weren't boats. I could see clearly now that they were breathing bodies. I also saw big faces, little eyes and smiling mouths. They were fish, bigger than I'd ever seen. There were lots of them, at least thirty or forty. Some of them were lying almost completely in the water, only partly visible above the ocean's surface. Others had their heads and bellies lying on the beach and lazily slapped their gigantic, flat tails against the shallow water. They all had enormous dorsal fins, and two side fins much longer than my arms, and some of those moved.

I stopped. I was so perplexed, I didn't dare to get closer.

"Why are the fish leaving the ocean?" I asked myself. "Is the ocean too polluted for them? Are they looking for food? Maybe they're sharks looking for human flesh. Not at all sweet like Tara's little shark. These were sharks with huge, razor-sharp dorsal fins like the ones I've sometimes seen from the coast." I thought about all the stories of sharks that bite off someone's arm or leg, just like that. I gulped. These fish were at least a hundred times bigger than the baby shark we'd seen on the beach.

I got even more scared when I heard something rustle behind me. Was it a shark creeping up on me to attack? No, it was just Tara.

"Look!" she said softly. "Whales. Those are whales."

She didn't wait for me, she just started out toward the ocean by herself. She looked tiny as she approached the gigantic animals. Some were as long as small fishing boats, others only as long as canoes. Tara was now standing beside one of the animals. She gave him a friendly tap on his shoulder and back. She wasn't scared, and the fish didn't do anything to her.

"I have to run home," I thought, alarmed. "I have to get Mom or Dad, and tell them to call the fire department. Or someone else. Maybe the park warden?" But I didn't go home. The beach was so quiet that my panic passed. This wasn't an emergency, it was a magical appearance, and it was beautiful.

I moved a little closer toward the beach, and heard the animals make clicking and grumbling sounds. Two of them lay on their sides, showing their grey bellies. Their sides had wavy, metal-coloured, yellowish brown or white spots and stripes, but their backs were solid black.

One by one, each looked at me with clear little eyes that had dark rims. They snorted loudly through the spout hole at the back of their heads. Some even spouted a bit of water, like a small fountain. A strange smell hung over them, an unusual mix of dry hay and bubble kelp.

"Don't they have funny heads!" shouted Tara across the wide back of one of the animals. "Just like a baby's round head." She came and stood next to me.

"I think they're pilot whales," she said. "There's a drawing of them in my book about the ocean. These are the whales that swallow bottles. If you want to send a message in a bottle, you have to send a lot of bottles, because half of them get swallowed."

She took me by the arm and pushed me right up to one of the whales. I watched the muscular mass move all over and contract and shiver. Then I went over to its friendly face, and didn't feel scared.

"Don't they look forlorn?" said Tara. I looked at her questioningly, because I didn't quite understand what "forlorn" meant. After all, the animals weren't wounded or anything. Actually, they all had contented smiles.

"They'll all die," she said, in a voice that didn't seem like hers.

"Die?" I asked. "What do you mean, die?" She looked at me as though I'd asked a very stupid question.

"They've beached. Can't you see that? They'll die soon, because they'll dry up. They're whales, don't you get it?" She said the word "whales" very slowly, as if she thought I'd never heard it before.

"Oh!" I said, and didn't dare to ask more, because she was clearly losing her patience.

"Beached," I repeated thoughtfully, and then it came back to me. The word "beached" brought back a memory from somewhere in the back of my head. It had happened once before, when I was very young. It was just as beautiful, and as sad. They were huge, much bigger than these animals, and their jaws were as large as boats. They were sperm whales, two of them. They died within a few hours. I watched them from Dad's shoulders for what seemed a long time. I asked him not to go too close, because I was scared. In a flash, I remembered the questions I'd asked then: "How can those animals just lie on the beach and die? They have eyes! Surely they can see the ocean behind them, they just have to turn around. Is the ocean too polluted for sperm whales? Are they looking for food?" The sperm whales got buried in gigantic holes in the sand. The belly of the first one burst when a crane lifted him. The entire place reeked of rotten intestines and sick blood for weeks after.

This time, there was a whole pod of whales, but so far they looked healthy. The animals just had to get back into the ocean. I quickly spun around and felt the panic I'd expected. I rushed over to Tara and grabbed her arm. She didn't wait for me to say anything.

"If the sun keeps shining, they'll all be dead by evening." She spoke calmly, as if she was planning to just let everything happen.

"We have to do something!" I shouted right by her ear. My voice was shaking, and I tried to clear my throat.

"What do you want to do?" Tara asked, and for a moment her temper threatened to flare up again.

"Throw buckets of water over the whales, so they stay wet. Call the fire department to push the animals back in the water."

Tara shook her head. The thin curls around her neck shook too. "I don't think we should. If the pilot whales want to die here, we should let them. If you try to stop them, then one day, they'll do it anyway."

"That's impossible! You don't know they want to die."

"I don't know it, but it's possible," she said steadily, emphasizing "know" and "possible." She lowered her eyes, and I watched her lashes touch each time she blinked them. "If your mother wants to die, you can't do anything about it either. Mothers who want to die, die in the end, no matter what you do."

She didn't say anything else. The fish on the beach were strange, and Tara too: she was calm, even calmer than when we used to swing together on the porch. She walked from one animal to the next, and spoke to them. When I heard what she said, I thought she'd gone crazy.

"Did you swallow my bottle?" she asked each one. "You didn't swallow my bottle, did you? The bottle has to go to Europe, you can't swallow it."

14

Suddenly, a great swell of noise rose from behind the dunes. At first, it sounded like the high-pitched buzzing of a lawn mower, but it became louder and deeper. I climbed to the top of a dune, and saw a jeep with big wheels lurching toward us at high speed.

It took a while before it reached the whales. It hadn't rained for a long time, and the sand was loose. On the door of the jeep it said DUNE WARDEN, and underneath it, in small letters, was written NATIONAL PARK BOARD. A man in a greenish brown shirt and khaki pants jumped out. He immediately started to run around and shout at two other men who also got out of the jeep.

"Thirty? Gosh, that's more than thirty. There are at least forty. And over there, about ten of them are lying in the ocean. How could this have happened?" shouted the man in the khaki pants. "I'll call the fire department and the police right away."

"Have the radio station announce that we need manpower. Anyone who can help is welcome," shouted the other, while the first went to the vehicle and started to talk into a microphone attached to a long cord.

"Hey little one!" shouted the other man — he looked like someone I knew — "Have you been here for a long time? How long have those dolphins been lying here?"

"For a while," Tara answered before I could say anything. It seemed to me as though they had been here for weeks. We'd been watching the animals for as long as I could remember, and we'd been talking for so long that it seemed as though I'd read an entire book about fish in sand.

"Yes, we just got a call over the air. An amateur pilot spotted them." Then he said to his friend, "How many are there now?

We need exact numbers for the preservation board in Boston. Those guys will be here soon with their trucks. We need to get organized."

"Forty-seven," answered the man curtly.

"Okay," shouted the dune warden from his jeep. He hooked in the microphone. "We're going ahead in our diving suits. Send those kids home. It'll get busy here."

I didn't want to go home, and neither did Tara. We took a few steps back to stay out of the dune warden's view. I figured, later on, he wouldn't care that we'd stayed.

"See, they're not whales!" I said to Tara nastily, while the three men unloaded black wetsuits and belts. "They're dolphins. That man said it himself."

"Im-pos-sible," Tara said positively, clearly hurt. "Dolphins are a lot smaller. It's in my book."

I pressed my lips together and walked away from her. I watched as the man who looked familiar got changed. He had a hairy chest and wore swimming trunks under his long pants. He wore a bracelet with a name plate around his wrist. It said ROBERT. He smiled when he saw me.

"You're Anna, eh, the little one from over there," and he pointed to my house in the distance. "I know your dad through work." I remembered then that I'd seen him with Dad. He got up and went over to join the other two.

Together, they waded through the water. The cold didn't seem to bother them. The dune warden signalled for them to go over to the small dolphin that lay farthest in the water. They pushed it toward the ocean as hard as they could, until its belly lifted free of the sand.

The men looked small next to the huge animal. We could hear them encouraging the animal, urging it to go back into the water. But the dolphin just drifted around desperately.

The dune warden came back to the jeep soaked, and started to unload buckets and some dirty white sheets. He filled two buckets with water and poured them over the animals lying right at the front of the beach. They hardly moved.

I went over to him. "Can I fill a bucket?" I asked.

Confused, he answered "Yes" without even looking at me. I went into the water with my shoes on and filled the bucket up to the top. On the way back, I dumped some of it into the sand, because it was too heavy to carry all the way to the farthest dolphins. Tara stood nearby. She didn't want to help, she said.

"Are these whales?" I heard her ask the dune warden.

"They're a kind of whale," he answered with a groan, lifting some heavy buckets as he spoke. "These are dolphins, but very big ones. They belong to the family of toothed whales. They are…" He didn't continue, because behind the dunes rose the sound of motors.

"Hey, little one," he shouted at me. "Stand on top of the dune and wave! That way, the helpers will know which way to come."

I waved as though my life depended on it. I saw more than just jeeps and trucks. People came marching across the dunes from all sides. Most of them wore hip waders and jackets. When I turned back toward the ocean, I saw three motor boats approaching. And I waved even harder, to the motor boats and the people in the dunes. Everyone who saw me pointed in my direction and increased their pace.

"They are whales," Tara snapped at me when I got down again. "They're toothed whales." I didn't even listen to her know-it-all voice. The beach got more and more crowded with people and trucks full of strange objects to help push the dolphins back into the ocean.

The dune warden had been talking through the transmitter in his jeep for a while now. He nodded and gesticulated, and talked loud enough for me to hear bits and pieces of the conversation — "when exactly " and "go ahead" Finally, he hooked in the microphone and went over to the crowd. He clapped his hands and shouted, "Attention please, people!" A few started to hiss, and gradually the murmur died down.

"Everyone, I want you to know that a biologist from Boston is on her way here. She specializes in beachings, and will bring a team of experts. Her name is Petr'Ann Jorssen. She gave me some instructions over the phone for all of us to follow. First of all: we won't bring a single animal to deep water unless we've taken a blood sample, and marked the dorsal fin. Only I will take blood samples, or the veterinarians Springs and Abbey. You can get tags here, but only these people will do the marking." The dune warden pointed to four men, two of whom I knew vaguely.

"Petr'Ann says we also have to weigh each animal, for statistics. I explained to her that, with our equipment, that'll be basically impossible." He rubbed his hands together, as if he was washing them, and thought for a moment. Then he continued.

"When we take the dolphins back to the water, we'll start with the biggest animals. If we take the smallest ones first, they'll get stuck again trying to be with their leaders." At the word "dolphins," I looked sideways at Tara. She stood motionless and watched a few small animals farther out in the water.

"We need ten people per pilot," someone shouted. A few people had already gone into the muddy water. I watched them take measurements of the whales' fins, their tails and their bodies. A woman in a diver's suit waded from one side to the other to take blood samples for the lab.

I went to stand next to a medium-sized animal, and I was almost sure it was female. She had the eyes of a huge antelope, and jelly-like tears rolled from the inside corner of one.

"You're crying," I whispered. The tears were as big as my finger. I tried to wipe one away, but the drop was tough, and didn't want to come off. I patted her round head soothingly. A clam lay in the sand right beside her fin. I picked it up and put it in my pocket for my shell collection. I also found a periwinkle and a cockle. It looked as if the ocean had spat everything out on the beach today.

A few men — still dressed in their T-shirts — tried to move one of the animals. The boats got as close as they could. A boy, not much older than me, threw a tow cable with a big canvas attached to one end into the ocean. The men in the water attached the whales to the boat by wrapping a sheet around each animal. The boats very slowly and cautiously pulled the animals out into the water.

"Hi, Anna!" I heard from behind me. It was Dad. He and at least eight other people were covering a whale with a large canvas to prevent it from getting overheated by the sun. I waved at him, and filled my bucket with water.

15

P̲etr'Ann Jorssen, the biologist, was tall and wore boots. Actually, she was incredibly tall, taller than Dad and Robert and most of the men on the beach. She had a ponytail, which made me smile, because the only women I knew who had long hair were on TV.

"Only little girls have long hair," Tara always claimed. "When women get married, they get it cut. But I won't have any to cut." Her hair was still thin and brittle. She wanted to let it grow, but it wasn't strong enough. I knew she was jealous of my full head of hair.

Petr'Ann gave concise orders. She talked much more with her lips than with her tongue, and it sounded to me like she came from a faraway country.

"She's from Europe," I heard Robert tell Dad. Tara stood right next to her. Next to Petr'Ann, she looked shorter than ever.

"We have to find the leader of the pod," I heard her say. "You measured them, didn't you? Give me the exact data, the length of each animal and how heavy it is. Then I'll be able to find it."

Tara hung on Petr'Ann's heels when she went to see the dune warden's list. Petr'Ann didn't pay her any attention. She talked and waved her arms. Everyone else on the beach watched and waited for her orders.

"Above all," she shouted suddenly, "don't make too much noise. These animals have very sensitive ears. Noise stresses them out." Tara tilted her head when she said that. She muttered something, and I tried to read her lips. Her eyes darted toward me, and when she saw me watching her, she strode over.

"Mom was stressed out too," she said, and went back over to Petr'Ann.

With Petr'Ann's expertise, things started to move faster. One by one, the shining, black animals were dragged to deeper water.

It took a long time, at least four hours, until they had all been pulled beyond the shallow water. Journalists took hundreds of pictures. People from the radio were eager to interview a few "assistants." Dad said something into the microphone, and I was allowed to say "Hi." The reporter asked, "How's the rescue going?" "Fine!" I called out, far too loudly. Then he asked, "Are you having fun?" and I said "Yes!" I knew my answers weren't original, but I was too excited to think of anything else. Tomorrow it'll all be in the paper, I kept thinking. The principal of my school and the boys in my class will hear me on the radio. My heart almost jumped out of my mouth.

Evening came, and the helpers were getting hungry. Nobody wanted to break, however, until every last dolphin was safely back in the ocean. It wasn't enough for them to be covered by the water. They had to be led clear of the beach. As long as they swam in circles like drunkards, they were in danger of beaching again.

They floated around desperately, and spouted up little fountains left and right. Most of the animals had gone back to their regular heavy breathing, and some slapped their tails flat on the water. Petr'Ann was out in deep water in a boat.

"She's busy with the leader of the pod," I heard someone say. If the leader finds its way, the rest will too, she'd said.

The pod moved into deeper and deeper water. The rescue crew looked on intently. Everyone was as quiet as a mouse. And out of the waves rolled the strangest shells I'd ever seen.

Eventually, you could see the shining body of a pilot only here and there, moving toward open water. They were so far away, you couldn't hear their noises anymore. My legs were tired and I sat down in the sand. The wind had dried out my lips, and when I licked them, I tasted the ocean.

Robert manoeuvred a low, humming boat toward the beach.

"Go home, men!" he shouted. "Everything's going to be okay."

"What about the women?" a woman in the crowd shouted. There was muffled laughter, and all the women who'd helped cheered. The next moment, everyone shook each other's hand.

People I didn't even know patted me on the shoulder and said I'd been a great help.

"Are you coming to the Cranberry tonight?" I heard Dad ask Robert.

"Yeah, I'll see you there. But I have to say, I don't trust it. It was too easy. If I know pilot whales, our problems are not over. Petr'Ann doesn't trust it either. She's going to hang around for a night, just to play it safe." The two men shook hands and walked away.

"Dad, wait!" I yelled.

"Oh yes, you're here too," he said laughing. He threw his arm around my shoulder.

"What about Tara?" he asked. I had no idea where she could be. I hadn't seen her for hours. In fact, I'd forgotten that she'd ever been there.

"Were those pilot whales, Dad?" I asked.

"Yes, those were pilot whales. They were big, eh?"

"Why did they lie down on the beach?"

"I don't know. People used to think they wanted to commit suicide. But now experts say it's because they've gotten lost. Their orienteering system gets confused or something." That seemed quite improbable to me.

"Don't they like their life in the ocean? There are so many of them, they can't be lonely. And the ocean is so big, there's so much room and there's so much good food they can hunt for. Why would they want to die? Or can they really be so lost that they swim up on the beach? When I get lost, I always try to retrace my steps. That often happens to me when I play in the dunes — sometimes I don't know where the ocean is anymore, or Truro — but I always get back. Don't the pilot whales have a mark in the ocean that'll help them get back to where they came from in the morning?"

"I'm not sure, Anna. Whales beach quite frequently. The last time it happened here, there were two enormous sperm whales. You were there too, but you were still very small. You probably don't remember."

"Oh yes, I do."

"Really? I remember it well. Already you had thousands of questions, but I couldn't give you the answers. If you get a chance, ask Petr'Ann. She'll have all the answers, for sure."

"Will she be at the Cranberry?"

"I guess so."

"Where's she now?"

"She's following the pod, together with a few people from her research team. I guess they'll all sleep at the Cranberry tonight."

As we continued our walk home, I suddenly glimpsed Tara sitting in the grass on the side of a dune. She was squatting, her face pointed toward the ocean. I didn't tell Dad I'd seen her.

Mom made both of us take a shower. I didn't feel like it, but Dad told me I could jump in with him. I liked the idea. He soaped me completely, and I soaped him.

"You're as slippery as a pilot whale!" he laughed. At the table, we told Mom everything that had happened. She'd followed everything on the radio, and had even heard my "Hi."

"Where's Tara?" Mom asked suddenly. "I haven't seen her all day yesterday, or today." I wasn't sure whether I should say anything about seeing her.

"She was with the whales, with me. Yesterday, she was just at home."

"That girl shouldn't be alone so much. Anton should look for a better solution than to always keep her with him," Dad said. Mom looked at him with a disturbed expression.

"She can't be here all the time either," she said. She added something in a suppressed voice that I couldn't hear. When she realized I was listening, she continued in her usual pitch. "Tony's very attached to her. After Tanja, she's everything he has. Without her, he wouldn't have survived the past few months."

"We're planning to celebrate the rescue tonight at the Cranberry. Not one animal died. We should have a toast to that," Dad said lightheartedly.

"I want to go too," I shouted immediately.

"You actually helped a lot," Dad said. "I think you can come."

"I think you can come too, *if* you bring Tara," Mom added. To Dad she said, "When you're along, I don't mind if they're together. Maybe you're right. We have to involve her more in what's going on, otherwise she'll never get over her mother's death."

Immediately, I didn't feel like going as much anymore. But I consoled myself with the thought that the rainbow man might be in his store tonight. I went upstairs to see if I still had money left over to buy a rainbow card. While I was looking, I heard the phone ring.

I rushed to Mom and Dad's bedroom. There was a second telephone beside their bed, and I lifted the receiver. I was too late. Mom was already talking with Uncle Anton. I held my breath, so they wouldn't hear me. I listened to their conversation.

"...ask something. Can I borrow a sleeping bag? I have a guest tonight."

"A guest?"

"Well, yes, a Ms. Jorssen wants to stay overnight as close to the beach as possible. She has to keep an eye on a group of whales or something. She was looking for a room with a view of the ocean, and our beach house is ideal. Robert came to ask. He was worried it wouldn't work out because of the death and so on but I told him I could handle it. A bit of distraction can't hurt."

"You're right."

"I don't have an extra set of sheets. That's why I need a sleeping bag."

"But Anton, you don't have an extra bed either. Are you going to put her on the couch or something?"

"I'm not sure. I'll manage. Don't worry."

"You can come and get a sleeping bag. And maybe bring Tara. Then she can come to the Cranberry with Anna. There's a party for the whales, I think."

"Tara. Why? Why does Tara have to be there?"

"Listen, Anton, Tara has to get out. What's the matter with

~ 79 ~

you? That child spends her time wandering around in the dunes or watching TV. You can't let that go on."

For a moment, there was silence. I was afraid they might hear me.

"Okay then. But she has to come home right after. And I mean right away. Everything has to stay under control now that she has no mother."

"I understand," Mom said. "See you later."

"Yes, see you soon." I waited for Mom to hang up. After the click, I put the receiver back on the phone. I went downstairs and stopped by the kitchen door to listen.

"That's what happens. The smart aleck didn't think it was necessary to buy more than two beds. He could've gotten another one for very little money. He's..." Dad stopped talking when I pushed open the door.

"Look," I called out innocently. "I still have some money left over for the rainbow man."

16

The rainbow man is Thom Klika. His store is right next to the Cranberry, and stays open until late at night. When you come in, you immediately walk on clouds, because the sky-blue steps, the floor in the store and the hallway are painted with beautiful fluffy little clouds. The inside wall of the store has a huge rainbow. As a matter of fact, everything Thom makes and sells has a rainbow: he has towels with rainbows, puzzles with rainbows, cups with rainbows. You can also buy a stained-glass rainbow to hang in your window, or one printed on fabric.

"Hi Anna!" Thom shouted when I came in. Before I greeted him and the door fell shut behind me, I quickly turned to see if Tara was following me.

"Hi Thom," I said casually.

"You look like you've seen a ghost!" he joked, and I thought to myself: I have. When Thom laughed, you could see another rainbow, because he had a colourful little sticker on his front tooth. I hung out a bit, and hoped Tara would leave me alone. I looked at the watercolour paintings and the calendars and played with the change Dad had given me to buy a Coke at the Cranberry. Put together with my own money, I had almost two dollars.

I chose a card with a rainbow that had really beautiful colours. Underneath it in small letters, it said that you can scratch the colours with your nail. Then you had to sniff it. I did that. The red bow smelled like strawberries, the orange one like oranges, the yellow one like bananas and the purple one like grapes. I didn't have enough money, but I knew Thom wouldn't mind. I read the card's message, TEARS DO FOR EYES WHAT A RAINBOW DOES FOR THE SKY. I didn't really know what that meant, but it was beautifully put.

"Were you on the beach today?" Thom asked when I got to

the front of the store. I nodded. He bent over and whispered, "Was Goody's whale there?" He let out a grim laugh. He looked like a phantom with his bald head and big eyes. "You can recognize Goody's whale by its tail. From it hangs a long chain with a lantern at the end. Goody hangs a lantern on the whale's tail, and rides it in the ocean. The fishermen think the light comes from the lighthouse, and lose sight of the north. Their ships get lost, and nobody knows why."

"I don't believe in witches," I said boldly, and put my hands on a silk rainbow pillow.

"You don't? You don't believe in Goody? Then you better watch out. Have you never heard her sing in the wind? And what about the phantom light on the ocean at night?"

"Goody Hallett's dead. The fishermen found her red shoes in the stomach of a whale." I slapped the card down on the countertop. I didn't feel like talking about witches.

"Is that for your mother?" Thom asked when I paid. I said yes, even though I didn't know who I'd give the card to. Maybe to Mom, but I also thought I might keep it for myself. I went outside sniffing the card's soft scents, and suddenly Tara stood in front of me. She still had the plastic bag in her hand that I'd noticed earlier. I didn't know what was in it.

"Show me what you bought," she ordered. Quickly, I put the card in my coat pocket, and walked past her.

"I've got my book about the ocean with me," she said. That changed things, of course. I turned back, and she lifted her book out of the bag. We sat down against one wall of the rainbow store. She opened the book at the page that had a bookmark, and together we read:

PILOT, OR PILOT WHALE

Toothed whale that lives in the Atlantic Ocean. The pilot is black and has a light-coloured belly. Its forehead is notably rounded. Its length varies between 12 and 24 feet. It lives in pods of 10 to 100 animals, usually led by an old male. Fishermen like to catch these animals for their fat

*and meat. Their thick layer of fat serves as insulation. The
pilot whale feeds itself on fish, squid and shellfish. It has
40 to 50 sharp teeth in each jaw (see drawing 16b).*

"How much does it weigh?" I asked Tara.
"It doesn't say, but I think it's incredibly heavy."
"Does it say anything about beachings and things like that?"
"Yes, here on page 36. Look!"

*Each year, groups of whales and whale-like animals beach
on the coast. Some experts claim that they lose their sense
of orientation due to an illness in their ear. Others claim
that the magnetic field of the earth causes it. Then there
are some who say the leader is ill, and that the whole pod
follows it. No one really knows the exact answer.*

"What a stupid book," I said. "It can't even answer our
questions."
"It's not a stupid book."
"But it doesn't even have the answers to our questions," I
repeated.
"I think I know the answer," said Tara. I looked at her in
disbelief and that made her angry. At first, she acted as though
she didn't want to talk about it anymore. But then she said,
"Really. I think the pilot whales saw something really bad in the
ocean. And that's why they don't want to live anymore."
"What do you mean, really bad?"
"I don't know. Just something really bad. Maybe an accident
with lots of blood, a fish that got stuck in the propeller of a boat
or one that's stuck between telephone cables on the bottom of
the ocean. Or a monstrous sea creature, a witch like Goody
Hallett. Maybe it's one pilot's fault that the pilot whales want to
die, because it talked about something it wasn't supposed to.
And because of that, it's being punished. The punishment is that
all the animals commit suicide, so that it's left by itself, completely alone for the rest of its life."
"Silly, that's impossible," I said. "How could pilot whales

talk about something they weren't supposed to, when they can't even talk?"

"They can," she protested in a whisper. "Dolphins and whales have a very complicated way of giving each other signs. They can send all kinds of messages. It's in my book." Her voice sounded very strange. It seemed like she was telling an old story, something she'd told a thousand times before. I began to toss some pebbles. She rolled her eyes and hissed in anger.

"You don't believe me, do you?" she shouted, and scratched my legs with her fingernails. "You don't even listen to what I say. You just don't get it, don't get anything."

"Leave me alone. You're hurting me," I said and got up, because I knew she was about to hit me.

"You're just like my mother. She didn't get anything either. She never listened to what I said, and now she's dead."

"Let's ask Petr'Ann. She knows everything about whales," I said, and walked to the Cranberry as fast as I could.

"Okay guys. Let's take a break," said Petr'Ann Jorssen when we entered the small room beside the café. "We still have a lot of work to do tonight." She sat at a round table with a piece of paper in front of her. She entered some data into her lap-top computer. The dune warden put a folder full of paper on the chair beside her, and went outside. The folder said: WOODS HOLE OCEANOGRAPHIC INSTITUTE.

"Hi Tara," said Petr'Ann when she noticed us.

"She knows Tara's name!" I thought in a panic.

"Did you bring your friend?"

Tara nodded. "Anna," she said, and pointed at me.

Petr'Ann turned to Tara again. "You're Anton's girl, aren't you? I just talked to him over the phone. I heard about your mother. My condolences..."

Tara didn't look at her. "Why do whales beach?" she asked promptly. Petr'Ann crossed her long legs and leaned back.

"Pilot whales have a very special system in their head that they use to 'see.' They send out signals we can't hear, and then listen for the echo of their signals. If it comes back quickly, then an object is nearby. If the echo isn't picked up for a long time, nothing's in the way." She picked up a pencil and started to draw. She drew a fish, with long lines coming out from it for signals. She also drew the ocean and the beach.

"If there's a flat beach in front of them, without rocks or cliffs or anything, they think that it's the open ocean. The leader swims onto the beach, and a few animals follow. They get stuck and start calling for help. Pilots are very social animals. They'll try to help each other, but the helpers get stuck too."

"See!" I said to Tara in a slightly reproachful tone.

"Did Tara have a different explanation?" Petr'Ann asked.

"Tara said they'd seen something in the ocean that made them not want to live anymore. Tara always has a very strange explanation for everything. She thinks whales can talk to each other and say things they shouldn't." While I talked, Tara carefully took the pencil and started to draw over Petr'Ann's sketch. She drew a bottle in the water. It looked a bit like a crooked fish, but it was clearly a bottle. It floated half above water. One fifth of it was filled with sand.

"She also thinks whales swallow bottles," I said quickly.

Petr'Ann smiled.

"Sometimes they do. But then it's by accident." Tara's face froze into a strange sneer when she said that.

"There are other reasons why whales beach," the biologist continued. "Sometimes they have parasites in their ears — worms, for example — that hinder them in listening for the echoes. Sometimes a storm confuses them. They lose their wind direction, and that can be fatal. But I don't think it's because they saw something awful, Tara. Why did you think that?" Tara pressed her lips together. She wiggled her feet.

"You're from Europe. I can tell by the way you talk," she said. Petr'Ann nodded and smiled. Tara continued, "In Cleveland, someone from Europe lived below us, and talked just like you. He was from Germany."

"That's not where I'm from. I'm from a country around there. I lived in Antwerp, a city in Belgium."

"Is Antwerp by the ocean?" Tara asked quickly.

"Yes and no. It's by a sea arm."

Tara pointed at the drawing. "Do you ever find bottles with messages in Antwerp?"

Petr'Ann didn't get the chance to answer. Robert arrived and started to talk right away.

"Everything's fine, Petr'Ann. Your equipment's set up in the beach house. You have an ocean view. Anton Myrold doesn't mind you staying there." Tara was surprised when her father's name was mentioned.

"Lucky you," I whispered to her. "She's going to stay overnight at your house."

Tara frowned and shook her thin hair. "We only have two beds," she shouted. "You can't sleep with my dad. Only married people do that." Her eyes were wild, and her fingers moved like birds that have just been caught.

Petr'Ann looked at Robert questioningly. Robert laughed. "Your dad said Ms. Jorssen can sleep in your bed."

"And what about me?" Tara asked with a lump in her throat.

"He'll let you sleep next to him, in the large bed." Tara closed down. She closed her ears and didn't hear anything else. She shut off her observational abilities. Nobody noticed. I was the only one who knew what was happening: Tara disappeared. She went into a glass tube to think. Maybe that was her beach trolley. I walked past her to the door to the café, because I knew she wouldn't talk to me for a long time.

"Anna?" Petr'Ann called. I turned around. "Will you shut the door? I want to talk to Tara." I slammed the door shut, and sat down with Dad.

17

People at the Cranberry had a lot of fun. They made fun of me when I came in, and made fun of Tara in the same way a little later, when she came in. She shared my chair, because there weren't enough for everyone. It was late, but nobody told us to go to bed.

"It's obvious," Tara said. "If you're older than twelve, you're allowed to stay up until after twelve." She drank her Coke, and I didn't get a sip, because I hadn't shown her my card.

Suddenly, a few people started to shush. All conversations died down. A man who had just come in said something, and a murmur filled the room.

"Didn't I know it?" Robert said. "I told you?" A few people got up and put on their coats.

"What's the matter, Dad?" I asked. "What's going on?"

"Anna, let's take Tara and go home. I'll walk you, and then I'm going to the beach. The pilot whales have beached again in the shallow water." I could tell by his voice that he was annoyed. It had gotten really cold, and it was dark.

"I want to help too," I said faintly, but I knew that wouldn't work. He didn't even answer. He just gave us our coats, and pushed us through the streets. Just after we'd left, Petr'Ann Jorssen rushed by. She didn't greet us. She wasn't wearing a sweater, just a polo shirt and her jeans. Together with Robert she disappeared in the jeep.

"Anna, I want to sleep with you," said Tara, bouncing the plastic bag with the book off her leg.

"With me? But Petr'Ann's staying with you. You don't want to miss that. If I were you, I'd want to be at your house." I couldn't think of a better argument. But Tara shook her head.

"I want to sleep with you. I don't like sleeping at home now that Mom's gone." I thought of the awful things she could do to me if I said no.

When we got home, Dad immediately went upstairs to put on warmer clothes. Mom told us that Uncle Tony had already called three times wondering where Tara was.

"Auntie, I don't want to go home. I want to sleep with Anna," she said, and her voice sounded like a kitten's. For a moment, Mom remained motionless at that sudden appeal. Is she acting, or does she mean it, I heard her think.

"It's fine with me, but your dad..." she started, but didn't say anything else because the phone rang. She made a swinging motion with her hand and answered.

"Yes, Tara's here now." Pause.

"How come? This late? In the dark?" Pause. Tara shook her head, and opened her big eyes wide.

"That's impossible, Anton," said Mom. "They got back half an hour ago and are fast asleep. I'll send her home in the morning." Pause.

"But, Anton, that works out well now that Ms. Jorssen's there. You were short of beds." Another moment of silence.

"No, come on. Forget about it. I'm not waking her up now. Tanja wouldn't have either." She hung up.

"And now go to bed. Maybe he'll come and see if I was telling the truth!" I knew she was teasing us. Tara thanked her quietly, snatched her plastic bag and carried it with her upstairs.

"Those men with the whales are lucky," I said while I took off my shoes. "The raccoons come on the beach at night. They break shells open, wash them and eat them. I wish I could go outside now." I threw Tara an old pair of pyjamas, and started to get changed.

"Turn your head to the wall," she ordered. I let out a deep sigh and turned around.

When we lay next to each other, she took the whale book out of the bag. I was exhausted, and didn't feel like looking at more whales. But she wanted the light on.

"I'll read to you," she said. Her head was on the pillow, and she held the book up. I turned on my side to read with her. I noticed sand in her thin hair.

"You didn't shower tonight!" I scolded.

"No," she said. I smelled sea salt and turned up my nose.

"I did," I said, "together with Dad. We soap each other and laugh ourselves to bits when we shower together."

Tara sat up and immediately asked, "Does he touch your breasts?"

"My breasts? Of course not, dads don't do that. Only boys do that."

"If people really like each other, they touch your breasts. It feels nice, that's why they do it. Your dad doesn't really love you, and that's why he doesn't do it." She clacked her tongue.

"Are you crazy?" I yelled, outraged. "That's nonsense. I don't believe a word you say."

She smiled and didn't say anything. She began to read: "'Studies show that the relationship between the mother and her offspring continues for several years. The offspring always returns to the mother, especially during stress situations, even when it's mature. Other female pilot whales also bond with the mother and child, especially when the mother is pregnant. The females protect the young pilots against the males, that can be very aggressive.'"

"What does aggressive mean?" I asked.

"That you want to fight and hurt someone," she answered.

I said, "I'm too hyper to sleep. Do you think they'll be able to rescue the pilot whales?"

"Do you know what I think?" she asked, and she waved her index finger. "I think those pilots are all female. The males chase them up the coast."

"That's not true," I contradicted her. "Petr'Ann wrote everything down, and she said there were males too. Why do you make up all these crazy stories?"

She started to whisper. "I'll give you money if you promise not to tell anyone what I'm about to say."

"How much?" I asked.

"A dollar."

"Where are you going to get a dollar?"

"From my dad. He gives me a dollar every night to be quiet. I can give you a dollar too if you don't tell." I moved closer to her. What was the secret Tara and her dad shared, that no one was allowed to know? A dollar a day, that was seven dollars a week, and thirty a month. That's a lot of money! I thought about her Mickey Mouse watch. I only had one watch, she had at least three. I thought about her bike and her beautiful clothes.

"Okay," I said. "I'll be silent as a grave if you pay me. What is it?"

She brought her face right up against mine.

"I think the pilot whales want to commit suicide, because..." she paused "... because they saw something awful."

"But what?" I asked impatiently, because she'd said that before.

"Well, they saw their husband and child play games together, very strange games."

"What kind of games?" I asked.

"Hmmm," she hesitated. "Games like boys do with girls. Like the father kisses the child, first on her cheeks, and then on her mouth. And then he lies down on top of her, and he touches her. And then — you know, those kinds of games."

"Pilot whales don't do that."

"They do so. It's in my book."

"But then how do you explain the fact that they commit suicide?"

"You idiot, don't you get it? You never get anything. I've explained it a thousand times before: the child told her mother everything, and the mother wanted her husband to play those games with her, instead of with the child. She thinks it's so totally awful...that she...doesn't want to live anymore. She swims to the edge of the ocean...and leaves the water. There, she dries up in the sun..." The end of her sentence sounded very shaky, and her voice went up. I realized she was crying again.

"Sometimes, when I'm alone, I have very strange thoughts. I think Mom isn't really dead, it only seems that way. I see her lie there in a plastic bag in her coffin, and she calls for help and gets furious. She bangs her fist against the wood of the coffin, but nobody hears her. Of course, she can't breathe for very long in that bag.

"I don't know what she looks like. Does she still have her clothes on, or did they take everything off? What about her necklace? I got her wedding ring. But she had another ring. Did they fix her hair, or did they just put an elastic around it like she did every day? I didn't see her when she was ready. Dad said, 'You probably wouldn't want to see her,' and I said 'I'd rather not.' Maybe it would've been better to check it out, to be sure. And also to say goodbye. The last time I saw her was at the kitchen table. I told a story and she told me I was lying. She said I imagined it and that it was driving her crazy. I kicked her leg and yelled, 'You don't get it. You don't get anything. You go on and on, and you whine, but you never get anything. You're the stupidest in the world. You're a rotten mother.' I said all that."

I didn't dare move. The book lay diagonally on her stomach. I saw her eyelashes move up and down very quickly. I'd never experienced her this way: the pilot whales were making her crazy. I'd rather have her punch me or pull my hair than have her lie there, with a broken voice and tears slowly soaking the pillow.

18

In the morning Dad told us the bad news about the pilot whales. He came into my room and sat on the edge of the bed.

All forty-seven of them had beached again. The rescue attempt was difficult, because it was so dark. The current in the bay was unfavourable, and Petr'Ann Jorssen had suggested they load the animals onto trucks. That way, the helpers could take them to the other side of Cape Cod, where the water was deeper with less of a current toward the coast.

Dad described how the animals, still half in the water, had to be taken out, and how the water was cold as ice. It had been so dark that their black bodies were barely visible. They were much more exhausted than they'd been in the afternoon. Their blood circulation had fallen below normal, and the dryness had damaged their skin tissue. Petr'Ann and her crew helplessly had to watch the mammals die, one after the other. The animals in the trucks didn't make it to the other side of the cape, and according to Petr'Ann, the ones left on the beach died of dehydration and maybe malnutrition. Of course, it was possible that they were already sick before the beaching. That would be researched.

"Did she cry?" Tara asked.

"What do you mean?" Dad asked patiently.

"Did Petr'Ann cry when the animals died?" she repeated in a shrill voice. Dad's mouth made a little noise.

"Does it matter?" he asked as he took his eyes off her.

"Are the animals really all dead?" I asked quickly, because I felt that Tara was bothering him and that he might leave.

"No, not all of them," he said. "Three of them were rescued. They're calves, I think young males, or, no — I think two males and a female — it doesn't really matter. In any case, Petr'Ann will take them to the New England Aquarium. She'd loaded the three youngest ones on a truck at the start, because she thought they'd be the strongest and would survive the trip. It worked, because the trucks are specially equipped. A few people from the crew went along to Boston, to the big care pool. There, the whales will be provided with good nutrition and can be watched closely. When they're strong enough, they can be brought back to the ocean."

We got dressed and went to the beach to watch. Dad walked with his head down and his hands in his pockets.

"Faster!" I urged him. He took bigger steps. Tara was a few metres ahead of us. She pressed her fists firmly against her stomach.

The animals were lying there just like yesterday, only they no longer moved. The little grunting and snorting noises had stopped, and the nervous tension underneath the slippery skins was gone. A sickly smell hung in the air, and from their bodies seeped dark fluids.

"Petr'Ann's still here!" I shouted.

Petr'Ann walked in between the animals with a book and a series of labelled bottles. She greeted us without smiling.

"I'm going back to Boston soon," she said in a hoarse voice. "Before I can leave, I have to record a few things." She knelt down beside the head of a pilot and looked into its spout hole with squinted eyes.

"Where was Tara yesterday?" she asked from behind the animal's back. Tara was still on top of the dune. The way she stood there, I expected her to spread her arms and fly away with the sea gulls.

Dad said, "She stayed overnight with us. When she got to our house, she refused to go home. According to Anna, she believes that the beach house is haunted. She's a strange child, but you probably already noticed that."

Petr'Ann got up and looked at him questioningly. She seemed to want to ask something, but changed her mind.

"Probably still tired too?" she said. He nodded.

"I'm not quite up to scratch yet myself after two hours of sleep, but duty calls," she said. She walked over to the next animal and took a close look at its eyes. Tara came storming down the dune. She ran toward the pilot, threw her full weight against its body and kicked it in the stomach. Its fat shook, and for a moment it looked as though the skin would break. She took a few steps back, came forward and kicked again, and again. She pummelled away at it like she was obsessed. With her wispy hair, she looked like a huge raging fly, one of those flies that keeps tapping its head against a window, harder and harder, convinced it can break the glass.

"Tara! Stop it!" Petr'Ann screamed. Tara didn't listen. Petr'Ann put her bottles down in the sand.

"Tara! Stop!" Dad screamed, and came toward her. She turned around and threw him a wild look.

"Go ahead, hit me," she said coldly. Dad stepped aside in surprise, and put his hands in his pockets. Petr'Ann felt the animal's stomach.

Dad grabbed me by the arm. He said to Petr'Ann, "I don't know what's wrong with her. Send her home when she gets nasty. My brother-in-law will deal with her."

He scarcely raised his hand, and waved goodbye. He pulled me with him up the dune.

"I'll manage," I heard Petr'Ann say.

"We're going home, Anna," he said.

"But, Dad, can't I..."

"Come, I said." I went with him, away from the whales, away from Petr'Ann and Tara who was always allowed to stay.

That morning, I didn't solve one crossword puzzle, and I didn't read one book. I sat in the living room and stared out the window. People passed by continuously. I knew some of them, others I didn't. They were going to see the corpses. The man and the woman with the knitted scarf came, too. The man's pant legs flapped like flags. At one point, I thought I saw Ms. Abbelese, but it wasn't her. It was another woman who wore the same coat and was about her height.

Petr'Ann drove the jeep to town and back at least three times. Each time, Tara sat next to her in the front seat. They both wore red sweaters, and looked like mother and daughter. From the bottom of my heart, I wished I had a dad like Uncle Anton. A dad who'd let me do anything and go anywhere. A dad who'd watch TV during the day, and let me sleep in his large bed at night. A dad who'd whisper things in my ear in public, and smile at me when I'd look at him. The wind was getting stronger, and the clouds moved in.

"There's going to be lightning," I thought. "Before long, the storm will slap water over the whales, and they'll come back to life. And then lightning will hit the beach, and Tara will be dead."

But there was no lightning. There was only Mom's voice calling that the soup was ready, and a strong wind that lasted for days, but never became a full-grown storm.

19

After the incident with the pilot whales, Tara and I were always together. Uncle Tony was busy with the cranberry harvest, and worked long hours. She'd come to our house for eggs or sugar, and was very friendly so she could stay as long as possible. Before she'd leave, she'd stand there pulling at her sweater, trying to think of one more story or comment so she could hang around longer. She was always interested in how the three young pilots were doing, and whenever Robert came to tell Dad, she was all ears.

Robert reported that the animals were gaining weight and gradually getting better. They were on a diet of antibiotics, vitamins, mackerels and herring, and they were being weighed once a month. It took twelve strong people to weigh them. Petr'Ann had given each pilot whale a name: one of them was called Notch, the other Tag and the smallest Baby.

"Ms. Jorssen asks about you. She says you should come to Boston sometime," Robert said. Mom nodded in Dad's direction.

"It would be good for Tara," she said.

Dad looked at Robert pensively, and said, "Maybe they can come with you sometime in the spring."

The prospect of the trip drove us crazy. Tara carried her whale book everywhere. She wanted to know everything about sea mammals, toothed whales, dolphins and pilots. She let me tell her about the ocean and the beach, and listened to what I knew.

"You can tell where the crabs are by the little piles they make. Like this one here. If I whip him out of his shelter, he'll take an offensive stance." With the toe of my shoe I dug underneath the pile, and whipped the crab up. We watched the small reddish brown animal get on his thin hind legs, and stick out his threatening claws. The next moment, he ran away sideways.

I grabbed a stick, and pointed it in his direction. He got a hold of it, and tightened his claws around it. I let him dangle until he let go.

"If you want to pick him up, push him in the sand first, like this, with your finger on his back. Then he can't get away. Lift him up by his shell." With a quick swoop, I caught him with my fingers. I showed her the crenated upper edge, and she laughed at how he struggled helplessly.

"He'll bite your finger," she shouted.

"He can't get to my finger. That's why I hold him like this."

"His eyes are peering out!"

I let him go, and he disappeared behind a rock as fast as he could. We went on, picked cranberries and ate them until our mouths were completely purple. Then we sat down in the sand.

"I want to read you something about the whales," Tara said. There was a strong wind, and the corner of her jacket flapped against my leg. Turning the pages was difficult. I rested my chin on my knees and waited for her to start.

"'When whales are in love and play mating games, they're not always nice to each other. The male bites the female and grates his teeth along her skin, sometimes until she's wounded. Therefore, the females often show fearful behaviour in the proximity of males.'" She rested her hands on the book and said, "My dad sometimes hurts me too, but afterward he comforts me. He does it because he loves me." I looked at her long fingers on the book. They were thin, and there was a blue shine on the joints.

"Why hurt?" I asked.

"Look," she said, and rolled up her dress. There were two brownish blue bruises on her thighs, and a few scratches.

"He says he likes me so much, he could lock me up, so that I'll be his doll forever. Then he pinches and scratches so hard it makes me cry. He says, 'You have to feel that I like you!'"

I grabbed a blade of beach grass and pulled it. The root was stronger than I'd expected, and the blade cut my finger like a knife. I licked the wound. The blood tasted warm and repulsive.

"Doesn't it scare you?" I asked. Her long eyelashes lowered. Her voice became very tiny and quiet.

"Yes, sometimes I'm scared. I don't know why he does it. He says all dads do it." She leafed through the book a bit more, but didn't read anything. "What do you think they did with the dead pilot whales?" she asked lightheartedly.

"Maybe they pushed them into the ocean, for the sharks," I said.

"Or maybe they hacked them into pieces to make sausages." We laughed. She told me about the crazy thoughts she has. Sometimes she thinks that Corn Flakes are really flattened and dried hamster turds. So when she eats them, she knocks on the box first and asks, "May I borrow some turds from you, please?" Or, after she dries her hair, she says to the hair dryer, "Thanks, hair dryer, for what you did. Without you I wouldn't have been able to dry my hair that fast." If the zipper of her jacket doesn't want to close, she thinks the zipper is angry with her.

"Then I let it cool off a bit, and it works again," she told me. She talked as if she really believed all of it. We got up and took our shoes off. The sand was cold, and my socks blew away. I grabbed them and put them in my pocket.

"When I was still in Cleveland, a guy from Germany lived right above us. He was funny. He painted stuff on socks and T-shirts, and then sold them on the street. He went to the movies a lot, and sometimes I was allowed to come. He was my best friend. He teased me a lot, but I liked it. He always made stupid jokes about my dad that made me angry sometimes. But overall, I liked him. I think he had a girlfriend, but I'm not sure. Once, I looked in his wallet. It had a picture of a cute face I didn't know. He always turned up his music really loud, and played the same record a hundred times.

"There were things he didn't like, and so he never did them. Like doing the dishes, or combing his hair. He liked to take a shower, and took one at least sixteen times a week. He always said he wanted to be famous. Then he'd want a sign on his door that said BEWARE OF DOG to keep his fans away. I would be the only one allowed in.

"His name was Henrik. He spoke American the same way Petr'Ann does, with strange gurgling sounds. He understood everything I told him. If I drew something, he understood what it was. Sometimes he'd say, 'Girl, when I go to Europe, I'll take you with me. I'll find a new father and mother to take care of you. A father who leaves you alone and a mother who helps you.' I always got angry when he said that, because I didn't want a new father and mother. But sometimes, in the middle of the night, I wished he'd take me to Europe."

I listened to her flow of words without breathing. She'd never talked to me for that long, and she'd never talked about her past before. The idea of a new, German mother and father gave me the creeps.

"One day, the police came to the door," she continued. "Henrik had to leave the country right away. They said he was in Cleveland illegally. He wasn't allowed to work, because he didn't have a green card. And they were looking for him in Germany. He left for Germany late that night without taking me."

She stopped and touched my ponytail.

"You have nice hair, Anna," she said. "I wish I had hair like that."

I wanted to say, "I wish I had long eyelashes," but it got caught in my throat.

"What did you say?" she asked. I took a deep breath.

"I wish I had long eyelashes."

Slowly she shook her head.

"Long eyelashes are bad," she said, and looked away from me. She took a crumpled piece of paper out of her pocket, and gave it to me.

"What's that?" I asked. It was a one dollar bill.

"Because you shouldn't tell anyone about the scratches," she said abruptly. She walked away in the direction of the beach house. I zipped up my jacket, and went home.

20

The fall went by slowly. After school in November, we watched the wind move the dunes and create a totally new landscape by morning. We counted the birds flying by, and watched the dancing windbags on the balcony.

"Remember when we still believed in Goody Hallett?" I said one free afternoon.

Tara nodded without looking at me. "And that story about little Filip. I gave you a piece of chalk, and it happened to be his hand. You almost turned purple out of fear, I remember that quite well."

I hadn't thought about Filip for a long time. Even Thom Klika from the rainbow store didn't say much about it anymore. I suddenly remembered the many evenings when David used to talk about the boy. He'd given me all the details and had named everything.

"The son who lived in the beach house had molested him. I think they mean, he did 'it' with a child. You go to prison for that," I thought out loud.

"He had to go to prison because he killed the child," she flared up. "Not because he did 'it' with a child!"

I moved away from the window. I didn't want to discuss it with her, because what she said didn't make sense.

"Look at the windbags," I said calmly. "They look like they've gone crazy."

On the second day of December, Dad brought the windbags inside.

"Otherwise they'll be completely torn to pieces by the time spring comes around," he said when I protested. He put shutters on the windows to keep the wind and sand out during winter storms. On our Christmas holidays, Dad helped us make wooden dolphins with loose fins that rotated in the wind. He sawed them out, and we painted them. When they were finished, we attached them to a long stick, and planted them in the snow. From the window, we watched the fins rotate in the wind. We watched them often.

On one of those quiet winter evenings, I was home by myself. The TV was on because I was bored. Tara had gone home long before, and wasn't coming back, because we'd had one of those fights we used to have. It was about one of my favourite pens, that she'd taken apart completely and couldn't put back together. So I stared out into the dark, when suddenly a conversation on TV intrigued me.

On the screen, I saw a girl of about fifteen or sixteen crying in front of her teacher. The teacher stood in front of the blackboard, and the girl leaned against a gigantic desk.

"He gets into my bed at night, when my mother's asleep," she said in a very small voice. "He started with his hands. He always puts his hands under my pyjamas and in my pants. Then he lies down on me. He hits me if I scream that I don't want to, and then he's sorry. He tells me I'm his favourite, and that he can't live without me. Then…"

"What happens then?" the woman asked. She was young. Maybe she was a friend instead of a teacher.

"His penis," the girl said without a voice.

"What about his penis?"

"I can't tell you."

I was speechless and moved closer to the screen. I could've sworn I heard Tara speak.

"He says it's because I'm beautiful. I wish I was ugly. And I'm not allowed to tell anyone. He always says that. Especially not my mother, otherwise he'll strangle her and drown himself afterward, he says. He'll leave me behind, all by myself, and it'll all be my fault. Because I didn't keep quiet. I'm scared of him. I'm scared that he'll hurt my mother and sisters."

She rattled on, and stopped now and then to blow her nose. I almost couldn't listen. With my toes curled up, I stared at the close-up of her face. My armpits got all sweaty, and it felt as though my intestines were sinking through the couch.

I kept thinking: Tara. Does Uncle Anton do that to you? Is that the secret he pays you for in dollars? I looked at the parts of my pen on the table, and wondered what we'd been fighting about.

The movie was interrupted by commercials for Coca Cola and detergents. I pushed the bowl of popcorn Mom had left for me aside, because there was a strange knot in my stomach. Fortunately, the movie ended on a positive note, with a nice stepfather adopting the girl, and the bad father in jail for the rest of his life.

I checked the program in the paper. The title of the movie was *Father Love*. "A film about incest," it said underneath. That night, I dreamt that Tara chased me with a big stick and stabbed me in my abdomen. Right after, she swallowed a whole bottle of pills. In the morning, she washed up dead on the beach. She had fins, and they took her to Boston in a truck. It was an awful dream, and I woke up in the dark. I was so scared, I kept the light on for the rest of the night. Outside, I could hear the fins of the wooden whales rotating in the wind.

That morning, Tara came over through the cold quite early. I saw her coming across the white dunes from far off. When she entered the kitchen, Mom and I immediately noticed that something about her had changed. Her hair was still the same, and her clothes, but somehow she didn't seem like the Tara we knew.

"Tara!" Mom exclaimed. "Your eyelashes! You cut your eyelashes off!"

Tara shrugged her shoulders. "For a joke," she said.

"Child, you shouldn't do that. Those scissors could get in your eyes."

"I'll be careful," answered Tara in muffled voice, and she motioned me to come upstairs with her. I followed her up the steps. I sat down on my bed, and she sat down on the chair that had my clothes on it. She threw my jeans on the floor. They were dirty anyway.

"Did you see it?" she asked. I nodded. "The same thing happens to me. Everything she said, happens to me too. When I was little he said, 'All dads do that with their little girls.' And he also always said, 'If you tell anyone, it'll be your fault your mother dies.' That's why I was so scared. And then suddenly it happened, and it was because of the bottles."

"The bottles?"

"I threw SOS messages into the ocean. I wrote notes saying I was in trouble. But then I got afraid the whales would swallow them all. I closed every bottle I found with a cork and threw it into the ocean. I wanted to tell somebody, somebody in Europe, maybe Henrik."

"Did you ever tell your mother?" I asked softly.

"I tried to tell her," she said, and emphasized the word "tried." "When I was little, I used to draw things about it, and later I told stories. She didn't understand what I tried to say. Just like you. You didn't understand anything either. It drove me crazy."

"Why didn't you just talk about what happened, instead of making those drawings?" I asked.

She laughed scornfully. I felt really stupid.

"Sometimes you try so hard to push things away that they're no longer there when you want to talk about them. I was also afraid Mom would go into another depression. She knew Dad loved me more than her, that's what made her sick. But it wasn't my fault." She looked around the room like a scared puppy. She looked like an old woman without her eyelashes.

"And then," she said shaking, "then one day, she came home when Dad was still on top of me, and he couldn't hide what we'd done. I cried and cried, because I knew something terrible would happen. I ached all over, and Mom was furious. For a least an hour, she screamed 'I am your wife! I am your wife! What's wrong with me that makes you take her?' She screamed it at least a hundred times.

"Dad went down to the beach, and I thought I was dying there in my bed, with Mom crying on the floor. I thought: Dad just wanted to scare me, because nothing will happen. And nothing happened. Dad came home again, and Mom went back to work. At night, Dad slept with me, because Mom didn't want him anymore. Every night, he lay down on top of me."

While she talked, she played with a small bottle of perfume she'd grabbed off my dresser before she sat down on my bed. She opened it, and the wonderful smell of chamomile helped me keep down my dinner. I'd never felt my intestines so clearly as when she told me the story about her father and mother. She put the cap back on the bottle, and continued.

"Ten days later something did happen. Mom went to sleep after four o'clock, and she had to get up to go to work in the restaurant. When I came into her room, she was just like a doll. Or like a pilot whale. She was dead, and every time I tell you something, I'm afraid someone else will die. Maybe my Dad, and then there won't be anyone left to take care of me."

I didn't say anything. Inside, I thought about the word "incest." I also thought about the dollar Tara had given me to be quiet. Would my mom die if I told Ms. Abbelese? Or David or Thom Klika? I shouldn't have taken the money.

"What happened to your eyelashes?" I asked.

"I cut them off, because Dad always tells me my eyes are so beautiful. I don't want him to like them. He says they are so beautiful he wants to kiss them, but I don't want him to kiss them." Without taking a breath, she added, "You know what really scares me? I'm afraid they'll throw Dad in jail, like the guy from the beach house and the father in the movie. My dad isn't bad. He's sweet and he loves me! He doesn't deserve to be jailed."

I grabbed the bottle of perfume out of her hands and inhaled the smell. She looked at her Mickey Mouse watch and jumped up.

"I have to go home," she said. "It's Saturday. Petr'Ann's going to phone soon." I sat up when I heard that name.

"Petr'Ann?" I asked much too loudly. "Why would Petr'Ann phone?"

"She phones me every week when Dad's gone bowling, so we can talk. Sometimes we talk for almost an hour."

"You never told me that," I yelled angrily.

"I don't have to tell you everything," Tara said in a vicious tone of voice.

"What do you talk about?"

"Oh, about everything. Especially about the pilot whales. Something's wrong with Baby. First, she thought he had round worms."

"What are round worms?"

"A kind of parasite, I think. He doesn't eat much, and he doesn't play with the others. Petr'Ann thinks he's younger than she originally thought. He should actually still be with his mother, but of course his mother died on the beach. She did an experiment with Tag. She wanted to teach her to take care of Baby. She called it an adoption. But Tag was probably too young to play mother. She clearly had no experience. She was a bad mother. Or better, a bad stepmother."

She put on her hat and pulled on her gloves. I noticed she was wearing another new coat.

"Will you tell me what Petr'Ann said tomorrow?" I asked.

"Okay," Tara said quickly, and then left. I watched her walk to the beach house through the snow. The big snowflakes came down diagonally, and her hat almost blew off. I sat down on my bed again to think. The whole room smelled like chamomile.

21

"Why does Petr'Ann phone Tara and not us?" I asked Mom when I got downstairs.

"She phones Tara?" she asked, surprised. "I didn't know that."

"She phones every Saturday, when Uncle Tony's gone bowling. Why does she phone Tara and not me?"

Mom clacked her tongue dismissively. "Petr'Ann doesn't have children and Tara doesn't have a mother. Maybe she wants to be a bit of a mother for Tara. You still have a mother. You should be happy about that."

I sat down by the window and pouted. There was always something exciting going on in Tara's life. Why didn't anything ever happen in my life? Time went by slowly, because I saw so many things at once. I saw snow coming down in crystals as big as the watery sun, sand that poked through the white cover like large cut diamonds, water that had formed an ocean from only a few immense drips of saltwater and shreds of evaporation that formed a pattern of clouds.

Everything was big and out of reach. I was the only one in Cape Cod who saw everything happen, but couldn't participate in anything. Life was boring. It would be a long wait until I was old enough to know what Tara meant when she said, "Sometimes there are things you want to forget so badly, you can't remember them when you want to talk about them." I spent the whole Saturday waiting for Tara to tell me what Petr'Ann had said. She didn't have a mother, but she had Petr'Ann. Mothers are the same every day, and incredibly boring.

I got the chills at the thought of mothers dying when you tell them things they're not supposed to know.

"Mom, at school they used to say that Goody Hallett turns

your mouth into stone if you talk about something nobody is supposed to know. I don't believe that."

"Neither do I, Anna," she said without looking up from the paper.

"Do you think somebody could die, because you let out a secret?"

"Anna, aren't you a bit too old for all that superstition? People don't just die. They die because something's wrong with their body, not because somebody else makes a mistake!"

I listened to the rustling of the newspaper and her loud breathing for hours. I solved all my crossword puzzles, and read my library books.

"Can I watch TV?" I asked toward evening, and I turned on the set. I watched a documentary about a faraway country, until Tara came into the kitchen.

"Tara!" I said, and noticed that my enthusiasm surprised her. She sat down next to me in front of the television.

"That's Europe!" she said pointing at the screen. "I can tell by the houses. They're all attached, and there are churches with steeples and weathercocks. Petr'Ann told me about it." I sat up when she mentioned Petr'Ann's name.

"She told me about her hometown, Antwerp. Her father and grandfather were skippers in the city's harbour. She came to Boston to learn about whales. Because there are no whales in Antwerp, she never went back."

"How's Baby?" I asked, and wrapped my arms around my legs.

"Not that good," said Tara. "They just put the whales in water tanks to prepare them for the ocean again. Or else, they might go into shock. They have to have a transmitter on their dorsal fin so that they can be tracked once they're back in the ocean. Petr'Ann says Baby's really having problems. He's gotten very shy and won't let anybody touch him. The biologists at the aquarium don't know what to do." She paused.

"I want to be a biologist too," I said.

"Biologist?" she asked. "I would never want to be a biologist."

"Being a biologist would be the greatest job in the world. I want to make nature documentaries, like those underwater films on TV. The only animals I don't like are snakes and rats. I read a book about India once, in which it said that snakes and rats kill babies. Even spiders don't scare me. When I see one, I don't squish him. I take him outside in my hands."

"Or her," Tara said.

"What?"

"Or her. You take *her* outside. A spider can be female, too."

"First, I scare Dad, of course. I pretend to put the little beast on his neck," I continued.

"Petr'Ann says you shouldn't be afraid of any animals. She says the only animal who can really hurt you is a human. You should watch out especially for those you love."

Mom slammed down the paper at Tara's last sentence.

"Let's eat," she said, and she started to make a lot of noise with the cutlery. She didn't leave us alone for the rest of the evening.

A few days later, Tara stopped me in the hallway at school.

"Anna, I want you to tell me a secret," she demanded.

"Secret? What do you mean?"

"I want you to tell me something, a story about yourself, something that's top secret that you're not supposed to tell anyone.

"I can't do that. I don't have any secrets."

She dug her nails into my arm and hissed.

"I don't believe you. I have to know one of your secrets, otherwise we're not even!"

I tore myself away and disappeared into my classroom.

22

Sometime in February, Robert phoned Dad to tell him he could bring Tara and me to Boston to see the pilot whales in the aquarium. For me, it was like going to the other side of the world, but Tara stayed very calm when she heard the news. She was often allowed to go anywhere with Uncle Tony, and she'd been to Boston a few times.

"Ms. Jorssen said for the girls to bring their bathing suits," said Robert.

"Bathing suits?" Dad exclaimed through the phone. "Why? I thought the Animals Protection Act didn't allow swimming with the whales, for sanitary reasons or something."

"That's true," Robert said. "Only Ms. Jorssen's having a problem with one of the animals and she wants to try something."

On the day of our trip, Tara had tied her thin fuzzy hair into a ponytail with a red ribbon. It made her look a lot older.

We were allowed to go in the jeep. The dune warden introduced himself as "Gerd." He sat in the driver's seat and Robert sat next to him. Tara and I sat across from each other in the hard back seat. I had to laugh a lot, because I was so excited.

"Don't laugh," she said, but a bit later she was giggling at the brown birthmark on Robert's neck. We drove for a long time. I watched the slow-moving traffic pushing along in our direction. My breath fogged up the window. My feet were a bit cold. Now and then we could see the ocean, but never for long. Tara showed me part of the new undershirt her dad had given her. I suppressed the thought of her thin body in that beautiful underwear, and Uncle Anton watching her.

I started to think Boston was as far away as Canada, but we finally stopped in a parking lot with a sign that read PARKING —

NEW ENGLAND AQUARIUM. The aquarium was a huge building full of visitors and fish. Normally, people paid to see the fish tanks, but we were allowed in free, because we were with the dune warden and Robert. We walked down a long hall with a gigantic window behind which squids, sea horses, jellyfish and small sharks floated around.

Tara stopped to see almost every aquatic animal.

"Tara, come on!" Robert yelled. She rushed over, but the next moment a lazy electric eel staring at us with its fat neck and charged body got her attention.

"Can you imagine how quiet it would be if you were a fish, with only the sound of water around you," she said.

"You're wrong," Robert answered quickly, and pulled her away by the shoulder. "Water is full of sounds. Fish communicate with a series of peeping, clicking and ticking noises."

Just before we reached the tropical fish with their colourful tails, the men steered us through a small door to the care pool. It was a strange, empty space. It smelled like dried beach grass in the summer, and there was this vibrating murmur of a motor inside the walls. I saw black shadows move at the bottom of the pool.

"Hi Petr'Ann," Gerd called up. Petr'Ann smiled and waved to us from behind the observation window. She climbed down along a narrow metal ladder. She stacked three buckets, wiped her hands clean and came over.

"Hi there girls!" she said cheerfully. I listened to her accent. "Glad to see you again." She put one arm around each of us and led us to the edge of the pool. The animals bounced up like corks.

"Ah! Here they are!" Three big heads started to nod at us, and from their spout holes sounded the strangest rattling and clicking noises. Notch got as close to us as the water permitted, turning on his side and reaching his head and neck toward our outstretched hands.

"He wants to be stroked," said Tara. She took a step back. I was somewhat scared too. I wasn't scared when the animals were lying on the beach so calmly. Now the pilots were as big and lively as sea monsters.

"Just tap his shoulder," said Petr'Ann. "He likes that." I forced myself to the poolside, and touched the slippery, cool skin. The breathing hole on top of his head moved weirdly, like a little rodent.

"He's smiling!" I said, louder than I intended. My voice bounced back from the white walls.

"Do you want to see Tag jump?" asked Petr'Ann. I nodded. She picked up the buckets and, through a small door, disappeared into the cold storage room. She returned with an obviously very heavy bucket. She shook the contents a few times, and scraped the metal of the bucket across the floor. Immediately, there was movement among the dolphins at the bottom of the pool. They all shot up at the same time, as if they were attached. They hardly moved, but with the help of their huge tails as a driving force, they surfaced in a flash. They spouted little fountains, turned on their backs and waved their pointy fins. Tara roared. The next moment, Tag jumped right out of the water, and dropped flat on her belly. The water splashed over the side and Tara's feet got soaked.

Petr'Ann burst out in laughter. She pointed at the red ball in the corner of the pool. Notch whipped it up and circled the pool with it. Then he threw it to us.

"Good boy, Notch!" yelled Petr'Ann, and she tossed him a squid from the bucket.

"Did you teach them tricks?" I asked.

"Not really," answered Petr'Ann. "The pilot whales are here for research, not to be trained. But dolphins are playful by nature. They love to throw things out of the water. Sometimes they stand up vertically, with their tail about three feet out of the water. Or they swim on their back, just for fun. In the open ocean they play with driftwood or rope. They also play with other fish, or with little crabs they dig up from the sand. If we didn't play with them, they'd be bored to death. But I think they like this pool."

Tag began to jump up and dive down, as if he'd heard what we were talking about. The other two followed his example. Tara went to the edge of the pool, and her jeans got splashed again.

"Just before, they looked like they were asleep, but they sure are awake now," she said.

"Dolphins only sleep three or four hours a day," Petr'Ann informed her. "They're probably only half asleep. The other half of their brain stays awake. They usually keep one eye open. They can only allow themselves little naps, because they can't breathe automatically. They have to come up for air regularly. If they don't, they drown."

"Strange, eh!" I yelled. "Fish that drown!"

"Well, they're not — " Petr'Ann couldn't finish because Baby had jumped up, and dropped flat on his belly. It seemed clear to me that they were back to normal now. Petr'Ann forgot she was saying something and started to talk about the water temperature.

"How many degrees?" asked Robert.

"Twenty. Or around that," she said. She asked us to sit down on the bench against the wall, so she could give Gerd and Robert papers they needed to take along to the Oceanographic Institute. A man named Roy Prescott came to talk to them. He was responsible for the pool. We heard him say that the animals would be loaded onto the Albatross IV in a few weeks. Researchers and some journalists come on the boat as well.

"If you want, you can come too, of course," he said to Gerd and Robert. "The boat's big enough. There's room for about fifty people."

"We'd appreciate that," Robert said. They talked about the transmitting equipment for a while. I watched the pilot whales, and clacked my tongue to lure them up. Soon the conversation caught my attention again, because I heard our names.

"Roy," Petr'Ann was saying. "The two girls sitting against the wall are Tara and Anna, whom I told you about. They're familiar with the animals, because they were at the rescue. The little one is very smart, and will understand what's going on. I think Baby will feel less threatened by somebody his own size."

I saw Roy look over at us out of the corner of his eye. He said in a low voice, "That girl is very small and delicate for her age.

It's worth a try, Petr'Ann. But watch the sanitary conditions, so we don't run into trouble."

"You know me, Roy. I don't play with fire," she said a bit louder, and waved her hand. She came over to us and said, "First, we need to take a shower." I sat up and grabbed the bag that contained my bathing suit and towel.

"Girls, I want to talk to you," she said enthusiastically. She squatted in front of us, her long legs folded underneath her body. She got so close, I could see the roots of her hair.

"Tara and Anna, you probably already know there's something wrong with Baby, the smallest dolphin." I nodded. Tara just looked at her intensely.

"It all started because of a bad arrangement. The guards of the seals in the pool next door allowed some drilling to be carried out in the mornings, for a new railing or something. Dolphins hate the sound of drilling. It must be unbearable to their sensitive ears. They got very restless and started circling around wildly. One afternoon, after things got quiet again, and the drilling had stopped, I went in the water for a routine check on the little one. Suddenly, the drilling started up again, I don't know why. In any case, Baby got a really big scare. Now he gets anxious each time I get in the water."

Petr'Ann turned her head toward the pool. Her voice was heavy, and her mouth sort of pulled crooked as she talked about Baby.

"It's such a shame. I'd do anything," she said absentmindedly. "Everything's gone downhill since that afternoon. He doesn't eat well and he doesn't want to be touched anymore. In just in a few months, he has to go back into the ocean. But if he doesn't want anyone to touch him, when we try to transfer him he'll struggle himself to death."

Robert, Gerd and Roy went to the computer room via the observation deck. The pilots surfaced now and then to get Petr'Ann's attention. She didn't react, and sat down beside us on the bench.

"Now you probably want to know why I asked you to come here," she said while she adjusted her watch. "I need someone who can calm Baby down. It has to be someone small, and that's why I thought of you, Tara. All the other guards here are men, and Baby doesn't want anything to do with them. You, Anna, could keep the other two busy, so they won't disturb Tara and Baby. You'd take in a box of toys they like: a searchlight, pieces of rope, balls and hoops." She stopped for a moment to see our reaction. I wasn't sure what to say.

"Do you want to do it? Swim with the animals and play with them? While Roy and I observe their reactions? It's important. I don't know what else I can do under these circumstances..." Her eyes widened while she waited.

Tara shrugged her shoulders and said, "I want to try it!"

Petr'Ann clapped her hands. "You don't think it'd be creepy or dirty?" Now she looked at me because I hadn't said anything yet.

"I think it would be fun," I said as I got goose bumps on my back.

Petr'Ann exclaimed, "Great," and she took us to the showers. "For sanitary reasons," she said. "The animals mustn't get sick. Tara, you go first, and then Anna, okay?" I was grateful she didn't push us under the shower together. Tara would've made me face the wall again.

I also didn't feel like looking at her naked body. It was small and bony like that of a grasshopper's. Even when she came out of the shower with her old-fashioned bathing suit and red T-shirt over it, I couldn't look. It reminded me too much of how she and Uncle Tony used to sit next to each other on the beach, both on one corner of the towel. It reminded me of the way Uncle Tony watched her, and of the many dollars Tara had in her room. But most of all, it reminded me of the secret in the bottles. It was a secret I'd shared for a while now, but one that gave me more of a stomachache every day.

23

Tara and I slipped quietly into the pool, and the animals clearly were very curious. Roy watched us from an underwater window, while Petr'Ann gave us instructions from above.

"Anna, throw the ball. Tara, move toward Baby a little. Reach out your hand. Don't make any sudden moves. He doesn't know you and doesn't know what you want."

"Do you snorkel?" she asked a bit later. Of course, we snorkelled. We snorkelled every square metre of water around Cape Cod in the summer. She gave us snorkels that were a little too big for us. Water got in until I tightened the rubber headband. I spat on the glass and rubbed it off with my fingers.

Now I could really see how big the animals were. They came toward me like sea monsters, and slid by like boats. I could feel the caresses of their movement, even when they swam six feet away from me. Their smiles made me smile. I watched them as they watched me, and we thought of each other as stranger than strange. They unnerved me with their strange crunching and clicking noises that sounded very dull underwater, or with their tails slapping.

"Easy," Petr'Ann said when I came up. "Take it easy. Don't make them crazy. Otherwise there'll be no stopping them. Move slowly." Tara was swimming in the corner, with Baby next to her.

"Good, Tara," I heard Petr'Ann mumble. I sat on the edge of the pool, and tried to keep Notch's and Tag's attention with the red ball. I was tired. The water on my lips tasted very salty. After some time, Petr'Ann jumped up and climbed down the metal steps to where Roy was following Tara's every move. I followed her to see what was going on.

"That looks good," Petr'Ann whispered while she kept her eyes on the spectacle. "This could work, Roy." I held my breath and watched this strange water ballet. Baby was lying still in the water, with his head toward Tara. Tara hardly moved. She only came up for air now and then. She looked even smaller than usual, and her movements under water were calmer than ever.

"Look how relaxed he is. We haven't seen him like that for a long time," Petr'Ann said. With a slow breaststroke, Tara moved toward Baby. Her T-shirt whirled around her like thin silk. Baby didn't back up, but stayed in the same place. Then he moved toward Tara. Now she began to get a little scared.

"Do you see that, Roy? Watch her behaviour too. She doesn't want to be touched either. I told you: she's just like Baby." But Baby didn't touch her, and Tara left him alone too. Her face looked rounder underwater, with its crown of wavy hair and the ribbon floating at the back of her head. Petr'Ann went upstairs.

"That's enough, Tara. You can come out now. We can try again later." With her wet hair, Tara looked as if she was bald.

We repeated the whole thing one more time that day. Roy entered everything on his computer: the number of times Baby came up for air, the number of times he circled around, the number of times he moved toward Tara.

"This could work," Petr'Ann kept saying. She said she'd call our parents. She wanted us to come to Boston during the week off, with their permission of course.

"It has to be okay with them. Working with pilots is completely safe. Dolphins are the most intelligent animals. Pilots are the most intelligent dolphins. This is the most fascinating thing you'll ever experience with animals."

"Am I dreaming?" I asked Tara when we were alone. "Or is this really happening?" This was the most exciting thing I'd ever done.

"I touched Notch," she said. "He felt like soft plastic."

We put our wet bathing suits and towels into our bags and walked to the jeep with Robert.

"I'll give you a call. Ten more days and you'll be here, if everything goes well, of course," was the last thing Petr'Ann said. She didn't wait for us to drive away, but quickly disappeared inside the building. It was cold in the jeep, and Tara crawled up against me.

When I got home, I didn't have to explain anything. Petr'Ann had already called. Robert held a long speech about how good it would be for us to help.

"Next time I'll take the girls to Boston," Dad said, "so I can see for myself what's going on there. I'm interested in dolphins too."

"What will Tony say?" Robert asked.

"I'll talk to Tony. Don't worry about that," Dad answered. Tara stretched out on the couch, and closed her eyes for a few seconds. I sat next to her and got a strange sensation. Just for a moment, it seemed as though she transplanted the energy of her nervous system. I felt her suddenly relax when Dad said he'd talk to Tony, and for the first time that day I relaxed too.

24

Dad took us to Boston on the first day of our week off.

"You couldn't have come too early. Baby's not doing well," Petr'Ann said even before she greeted us. She said a quick "hello," shook Dad's hand when he got out of the car and motioned us to follow her. While we were walking, she explained to Dad exactly what had to happen.

"The animals have to get familiar with the transfer to the ocean. If they're nervous or panicked, they'll swim too fast, and wound themselves or each other." She seemed like a startled deer: her hair was a mess and she stumbled over her own words.

"I stayed up with the animals all night," she said. "I'm exhausted. Sorry."

Dad only said "Mmmm," now and then, and nodded. I saw him take a deep breath when we entered the room of the care pool. I immediately went to the poolside. Notch, Tag and Baby shot through the water in a closed group. I'd never seen them swim that fast.

"They hardly rested last night. A real blow," Petr'Ann said. "They sense there's something wrong with the smallest one, and they're reacting to it." She smelled like coffee and sugar.

"Tara and Anna, you can go into the shower right away. But don't go in the water yet. They're too wild." We went into the shower — first Tara, then I — and came back barefoot and dripping. Dad and Petr'Ann were gone.

"They're upstairs," Tara pointed out. Dad looked at the computer screen over Roy's shoulder. But Petr'Ann was nowhere in sight.

"She's in the isolation pool," Roy said. "Together with Bert she's trying to separate Notch from the other two. He's so big that in his agitated state he pushes the other two against the side of the pool." After a brief pause, he turned to Dad and said,

"Those animals weren't meant to swim around in such a small space. If you ask me, they should've been taken back to the ocean weeks ago. But what can you do? Those research results, you know, everything's so important and takes so much time. They left me no choice."

On the far side of the observation deck, Notch was being lured to the other pool with a bucket of squid. He made a grating noise, and when he reached the bucket, he began to chatter. The tall man in shorts had to be Bert. He threw Notch a fish, while Petr'Ann distracted the other two animals with a lighter. She moved the flame from left to right, let it disappear and appear. Baby wasn't particularly interested. In the meantime, Bert closed off the isolation pool, and Notch began to explore his new space.

Dad kept asking questions, especially about our safety. Roy waved away all his objections. He talked about good-natured animals, no risks and constant supervision.

Petr'Ann waved to us from the observation deck.

"You can go," Roy said. "Don't run on the steps! They're slippery."

I went over to Dad and kissed him.

"I'll watch a bit, and then leave," he said. "Promise me you'll be careful. Do what Petr'Ann asks you to do."

I promised and climbed down the steps very carefully. The water splashed over the edge of the pool in small waves. The two animals stayed at the bottom of the pool, and only came up for air now and then.

"Listen girls," Petr'Ann said, and pulled us over to the wall. We sat down on the bench. "Today is the first day. So you won't stay in the water for very long. Anna, you stay with Tag. The best way to calm her down is by being calm yourself. Tara, try approaching Baby like you did the last time. You don't need to do anything more or less. He's more nervous than the last time and you'll notice he's lost a lot of weight. I'm worried about that. He's traumatized for some reason. We have to help him over it, otherwise he's in real danger." She paused.

"We'll also watch for your safety. Never enter the pool when you're alone with the animals. The water is the dolphin's domain, no matter how well you can swim." She massaged her upper arm while she spoke, rubbing until her skin turned red. She also blinked her eyes a lot.

"Let's go," she said. We got up, and slipped into the water close to the wall. The water was as warm as that in a swimming pool.

"Easy!" Petr'Ann yelled. "Tara, wouldn't it be easier without that T-shirt?" I choked when she asked that. "Don't ask that. She'll kill you," I wanted to say. But Tara stayed calm. She laughed amiably and shook her head.

"That T-shirt won't make any difference," Tara grumbled. "You better get that red ball out of the water." She pointed at the ball in the corner of the pool. Petr'Ann picked it out without hesitation and threw it in the wall closet.

"Easy!" I said teasingly. She smiled apologetically, and closed her eyes. I spat in my diver's mask, put it on and swam. Tag and Baby rose up like shadows. Their tension was noticeable in the current: I felt it in my ear drums, although I don't know how. I wondered if they recognized me.

"Time to go to sleep," I said in my thoughts. Dolphins don't sleep. If they sleep, they'll drown, I remembered. "Quiet! Quiet!" It didn't help. Their round heads kept shooting past me, then past Tara, and then to the bottom of the pool again. I was getting cold because I hadn't moved. "Easy. Easy," I kept repeating. It seemed to take hours before they slowed down and stayed in one place to look at us.

"Baby's probably about twenty months old," Petr'Ann said after we were dressed again and watching the animals through the glass walls of the pool. "Young dolphins sometimes stay with their mothers until they're five years old. You have to under-stand that the beaching and the stay in this pool have confused him. In the beginning, solid foods didn't sit well with him either. It was pretty clear. He always wanted milk, and looked for nipples on Tag. I was hoping that Tag would adopt him, but she was too young. She's never been a mother. She has no idea what to do with a young." Notch started to scream.

"He's not happy with his separation," Petr'Ann said. "Pilots are real herd animals. We shouldn't actually be allowed to do this but there's no other solution. You should've seen Baby yesterday. He swam with his tongue hanging out of his mouth, and released big air bubbles. They swam so fast that Tag decided to swim in between Baby and the wall. She was trying to prevent Baby from constantly hitting the side. They made quick sharp turns, and sometimes you could hear Tag's skin scrape against the wall. A horrible sound. I couldn't stand it, especially when she peeped out of pain." Her face looked as if she had bitten into an orange pit.

"They were egging each other on. Notch constantly dealt out blows with his tail. He couldn't stand the stress. They know how each other feels. They feel Baby's dissatisfaction, and that spoils the whole atmosphere." She got up with a sigh that came from deep in her chest.

"But I'm not hopeless. Baby has calmed down a bit since you got here. You provide a distraction, and that's good for him. At least I hope so." She grabbed her coat and rolled it up.

"Let's go home," she said. "Bert's staying for a while. You're probably hungry." She drove us to her apartment on the other side of the city. The spare bedroom had two mattresses on the floor, a dresser in the corner and a lamp. The wallpaper pattern looked like a wild array of flowers at first sight, but when I looked closer, I could see hundreds of islands surrounded by a deep blue ocean.

At dinner, Petr'Ann told us all kinds of remarkable stories about dolphins and whales. We listened with our mouths wide open. She knew the most remarkable legends and myths from other cultures, and showed us the books in which she'd found them all: "The Maori people live in New Zealand and they believe that when someone dies, his or her soul travels to the most northern point of the island, and gathers with all the other spirits and souls under a gigantic tree on top of a cliff. They wait until night falls, and then dive into the bay together. When they hit the water, they turn into dolphins. At least, that's what they believe. There are people who are convinced that dolphins have telepathic abilities, that they can read your thoughts, and cure illnesses. I don't know what's true and what's not, but I do know those pilots are the smartest creatures I've ever been around. Who wants another piece of herring?"

"Smarter than dolphins?" Tara asked.

"Pilots are dolphins. They belong to the family of dolphins. And dolphins are whales. Most people think only the tumblers are that intelligent, and that's because you only see tumblers at work in zoos and dolphinariums. They're not that big and don't protest at being imprisoned. But there are other dolphins who are very smart. I once worked with an orca in California. Those animals are so big they could flatten you during a moment of absentmindedness. But they're not intentionally dangerous. Even though they have sharp teeth and are real predators." She showed us a picture with a group of orcas attacking a baleen whale and tearing pieces of meat from its body.

"Ugh, the ocean looks red with blood," Tara moaned.

"Did you want another piece of herring?" said Petr'Ann, unfazed. I shook my head.

"My dad hates herring," I said. "He always says, 'All those bones! I'd rather eat a brush.'"

Petr'Ann laughed and wiped her mouth. "We don't know a lot about most dolphins, because it's so difficult to study them in their natural surroundings. They're so fast and there are tens of different kinds."

Tara put her hands together. "Can they all read each other's thoughts?" she asked. Petr'Ann shrugged her shoulders.

"They definitely have very well developed sense organs. With their echo system they can see right through things, so to speak. They can distinguish various metals, or see what hides underneath the sand."

"Great," I moaned. "I wish I could do that."

Tara bent across the table as far as she could. "Can they read our thoughts too?" she asked in the voice of a conspirator.

"It seems that something changes in your glands when you're happy or sad. People say dolphins can sense those changes. Experiments have been done with autistic children: the animals seemed to understand perfectly what went on inside those children. I don't know how it works either."

"I know how it works!" Tara exclaimed. "Dolphins are people's souls, and souls see everything." She laughed when she said that, but I knew she partly believed it.

"You could be right," Petr'Ann said as she stacked the plates and scraped the bones together. "People usually don't see what they should see. And then, when they do clue in, they die." I saw her look at Tara from the corner of her eye as she said that. Tara stared at the bottle on the table and didn't say anything.

25

The next morning, Tara asked something she'd never asked before: "Anna, can I wear your white T-shirt today? Instead of my red one?"

"What's wrong with your red one?"

"It's not good for Baby. It confuses him. Dolphins are like people. Petr'Ann said it herself yesterday. I scare Baby with that red T-shirt." I tossed her my T-shirt, and put my shoes on. She faced the wall while she got dressed. It was the first time she didn't make me turn away.

"There's a bump in my mattress," she grumbled. The white T-shirt didn't look as good on her as the red one, but I didn't let on. She pushed on the bump in the mattress with both hands.

"Doesn't do anything," she said, and sat down. I opened the window.

"Did Petr'Ann say when we need to be ready?"

"I don't know. I think we're up too early. Everything's still quiet." She looked at herself in the mirror. "I wish I had a green T-shirt. That would be the best for Baby."

I sat down next to her on the mattress, and definitely felt the bump. She pulled in her legs and said, "You know, I was think-ing about you and your dad yesterday. He kissed you on your mouth when he left. My dad does that too, but I hate it. With you it looked like fun and completely normal. Even when he slaps your thighs and holds you." Her eyelashes had grown back and looked longer and darker than ever. "It makes me think: there are two kinds of touching. Touching you find normal, or fun, and the kind that makes you feel uncomfortable."

I got goose bumps on my neck. Why did she always have to talk about her dad? And on top of that, compare her dad to mine? I went to rinse my mouth in the sink. She ignored me and continued.

"It has to do with your body, or, actually, with parts of your body. There are green body parts that everybody you know can touch. I mean your hands and feet and so on. Then there are the orange body parts: your mouth and your neck and your thighs. Only a few people are allowed to touch them. The red body parts, nobody is allowed to touch, because they're yours only, completely private. You can imagine what they are."

"Your vagina, for example," I filled in.

"Your what?" she asked with a nervous laugh. "What did you call it?"

"Your vagina," I repeated, blushing.

"Do you mean...?"

I nodded. "Don't be stupid," I said. "That's completely normal. Mom used to say 'pee hole.'"

"My mom never talked about those things," she said looking away. "I think I hear Petr'Ann. Let's talk about something else."

There was shuffling in the room next door. It lasted a few minutes before it was quiet again.

"Do you think Petr'Ann knows the story about Goody Hallet?" Tara asked suddenly. I shrugged my shoulders.

"Maybe we should tell her. It's..." She stopped, because the next moment we heard a soft thump that came from below us. Then again and again. The sound had a beat to it, and we listened intently.

"A poltergeist," I said jokingly. "That's what you get, when you talk about witches." I thought about the many creepy evenings in the dunes with David. Tara got up, left the room and knocked on Petr'Ann's door.

An hour and a half later, we were back in the water with the animals. I don't know whether the T-shirt made a difference, but Baby was calmer than the day before. Even so, Petr'Ann advised us not to move very much, just glide back and forth, and throw a ball once in a while. After about twenty minutes, I sat on the side of the pool shivering.

"I'm cold, Petr'Ann," I said.

"Put a towel around your shoulders until you're warm again," she said. I was too lazy to move. I watched Tara put her hand on Baby's side now and then. She touched him like you touch a book you don't want to get dirty, with just her palms, and her fingertips bent upward. He let her, but never for long.

"Anna, why don't you get dressed. You're shivering." Petr'Ann rubbed me dry quite roughly. A bit later, Tara, completely dressed, sat down beside me.

"Baby's got something," she said. "Something around him that calms me down. I could go to sleep now."

"He hypnotizes you!" I said.

"Maybe. Or maybe I'm just tired from swimming." She went in the water a few more times that day. And when she wasn't in the water, she watched Baby from the side. He surfaced once in a while, and chattered through his spout hole. But usually, he was preoccupied with himself.

On the lower observation deck, Roy Prescott was constantly counting. Now and then, he called out something to Bert or Petr'Ann: "Breathing rhythm: seven times a minute," or "Has been taking advantage of Tag's turbulence for nine minutes now."

"It's getting better, but he's still not eating enough," Petr'Ann said. "I'll be able to sleep better tonight." The dolphins began to whistle when she turned off the lights.

"They don't want us to leave," she said.

"Do they like us?" Tara asked.

"They always whistle when we turn the lights off at night. But they probably also like you."

On the drive home, I sat by the rolled-down window with wet hair. The draft gave me the sensation that my head was full of dolphin water.

In the hall, between the sets of glass apartment doors, a little girl played with a ball.

"This is the caretaker's little girl," Petr'Ann said. The girl greeted us shyly. The ball bounced from the wall to the floor. I recognized the sound.

When we returned to our wildly coloured room, we noticed the window still open. The curtain didn't move.

"Have you noticed?" Tara asked. "There's no wind."

"Maybe the city stops the wind?" I suggested, because I couldn't imagine a city on the coast without wind.

"Normally, it is windy here!" Petr'Ann called from the hall. She took some clothes out of the closet.

"There's even a mosquito here!" Tara screamed. "Our mosquitoes fly inland right away. I'll be covered in bites tomorrow." She tried to hit the insect with her towel, but missed. The next moment he was gone.

"Did I get him?" she asked.

"There!" I pointed. She slammed the beast flat against the wall. His body hung from an island that, according to the letters on the wallpaper, was called "Preree."

"There, you ugly monster. You're dead," she yelled.

Only then, I noticed Petr'Ann watching her through a crack in the door.

26

While Tara was still in the water with Baby, Petr'Ann called me over. She sat on a fake leather couch on the observation deck, and looked at me pensively.

"How are you doing?" she asked. I nodded that everything was fine. I knew something was up. She pointed at Baby in the water and said, "Baby just ate the way he should be eating for the first time. He likes being fed by someone small, I guess." She went over to the small table and took a sip of coffee that was getting cold.

"Anna, do you know why Tara always keeps her T-shirt on when she swims?"

The question scared me, and I looked at my fingernails. They were whiter than I'd ever seen them, and as soft as Mom's after doing the dishes. I shrugged my shoulders.

"Does she not want anybody to see her bathing suit?" She was calm, which made me suspicious.

"Her bathing suit's incredibly out of date," I said. "She doesn't want anybody to see it."

"Does she often wear clothes that are out of date?" she asked.

"No, only an out-of-date bathing suit. She gets all her other clothes from her... father. Everything's new and trendy." I didn't want to choke at the word "father," but it happened anyway. I quickly looked away, and smiled at Roy downstairs, who walked beside the pool.

"Doesn't her father want to buy her a trendy bathing suit?"

"Yes, he does. Very much so. He buys her a beautiful bathing suit every summer. But Tara gives it to the other girls in her class. She only wants to wear that old black bathing suit." Petr'Ann nodded very slowly. I bit my lip, because I didn't know what she was thinking.

"I guess it just feels comfortable," I added quickly. Then I shut my mouth. "I won't say another word," I thought to myself.

"Come and sit with me for a minute," Petr'Ann said with a strange sweetness. I sat down reluctantly. "Anna," she said again. "Has Tara ever told you that she thinks she's dirty?" I slowly shook my head.

"No," I said. "She's never said that. Well, maybe once when she'd fallen in the mud. Why would she think she's dirty?"

"Oh, I don't know. No reason, really. She's so closed. I don't know anything about her. It's much easier to talk to you." It was a trap! I knew it and suddenly I felt like a snail. I felt like someone who should talk, but is too slimy to move or open her mouth. I remembered the picture of a snail crawling along the edge of a razor blade.

"That's possible," Ms. Abbelese had said. "Snails are so slimy that they don't feel any pain, and don't get wounded either."

I was exactly like that snail on a razor blade, when I sat beside Petr'Ann on the couch. I felt something cut across the entire length of my stomach. Even though I wanted to leave, I couldn't, because I was stuck to the couch with my own slime. I sat and waited for her next dreadful question. Tara came up for air, and disappeared immediately afterward.

"Remember that night at the Cranberry? I wanted to talk to Tara, but she didn't say anything. She closed down. Remember we talked about those bottles? She threw bottles with messages into the ocean. Remember?"

I nodded, because a snail can't talk, just nod.

"Do you know what the message in the bottle was, Anna?"

I said, "No." Much too fast for it to be true.

"Honestly?"

"Honestly," I said, and the blade stung my stomach.

"Anna, I think I know what the message was. Somebody had to come and help her, right?"

I didn't nod. My head was so heavy, it almost fell off. "Don't say anything," I said to myself. "Tara will go crazy if I say anything. The secret is too horrible. I can't talk about this. The secret is too horrible."

I quickly gasped for air and said, "That's because she was scared of Goody Hallett. Goody Hallett used to live in her house. And whenever she heard the wind, she thought it was Goody Hallett. But that was when we were small. Now, we don't believe in witches anymore."

"Is Goody Hallett a witch?"

"More like a mermaid. She used to ride on the back of a whale, and caused ships to sink or run ashore with her lantern. But mermaids aren't real either." I talked excessively, because this was something I could talk about without feeling the pain in my stomach.

"Do you know where the myth of the mermaid comes from?" she asked. "Sailors used to see dolphins in the ocean during trips that would last for months. The animals were so sweet and elegant that, from afar, they resembled beautiful women with fish tails. That's how all those wild stories about mermaids and sirens came about."

"Really?" I said. "How interesting!" I scrambled up to get away. I didn't want to hear that Goody Hallett was really a dolphin.

"Sit for a minute," she said quickly. I was getting feverish in that boiling-hot observation room that was starting to resemble a greenhouse more and more.

"You know, Anna," she said. "Tara thinks I found the bottle with her message in Europe. I mean, she doesn't *really* believe that, but part of her wants to. She wants somebody to help her solve her problem. I want to help her, and so do you. We have to work together to get anywhere."

"Work together," I echoed, to gain time. It was so hot that the objects around me moved, and seemed to melt like ice.

"I've often talked with Tara over the phone. She doesn't say anything, but gives signals. I also saw the situation at her house, and found it all quite strange. Once she briefly told me about Goody Hallett. She said she used to be scared of the seawitch, because she could turn your mouth into stone if you talked about something no one was allowed to know. I remember quite well what she said after that. She said, 'I don't believe in Goody anymore, because my mouth hasn't turned into stone. I told Anna something today that no one was allowed to know, and my mouth hasn't turned into stone.' I said, 'What did you tell her, Tara?' She got very quiet on the phone and said, 'Oh, just something about a movie I saw. She's my best friend, you see. I tell her secrets only she's allowed to know. Then I give her a dollar, so she won't tell anyone. We have fun playing that little game.' That's exactly what she said. I'll never forget it. At that moment, my suspicion was confirmed. A little later, we talked about being scared of animals, and I told her she doesn't have to be scared of any animals. 'You should only be scared of humans,' I said, 'because they can really hurt you.'"

I remembered Tara telling me something along those lines after a phone conversation with Petr'Ann. But I didn't have the time to recall the situation. I heard a noise that made me break out in a cold sweat. "The wind!" I thought, alarmed. "The wind's back. I hear Goody Hallett!" I heard the wind for the first time in Boston.

"I haven't been scared of Goody Hallett for a long time," I said. I could tell by the expression on Petr'Ann's face that she didn't know why I'd said that. I didn't know myself. I reached for my mouth and touched my lips. They had turned into stone. I had changed into a snail with lips of stone.

"Anna, just tell me what you know."

"If I say anything, something's going to happen," I said weakly.

"Anna, nothing's going to happen. I'll take care of it. Tell me what you know." Tara stood at the side of the pool and waved at us. For a moment, it looked as though she'd dry herself off and join us. But she dove into the water head first. My lips relaxed again.

"Uncle Tony," I muttered. The glass walls of the observation room caved in on me. Now I could feel the cutting feeling everywhere, even in my neck and on my back. I had to inhale deeply to get rid of it. "He — he does something to her. Then he gives her a dollar. So she doesn't talk. He says, he likes her so much, he has to do it..." Again, I inhaled deeply.

"When Aunt Tanja found out, she swallowed a bunch of pills. Tara thinks it's all her fault. She cries a lot. She cries when I'm there and she cries when I'm not there. She never used to. She never used to cry — but she'd curse and rage and kick me in my stomach. Then, I didn't know why, but I do know now. It's a horrible secret. It drives both of us crazy. I don't want to hear anything more about it, because it's making me ill." My words fell out of my mouth like vomit. I had never talked like that, hardly breathing — although I'd tried — and with that pain in my stomach.

Petr'Ann watched me like a frozen TV image. I knew she was older than I'd imagined, maybe even older than forty.

"I thought so. I thought so," she said a few times in a hoarse voice. "I suspected it when she didn't want to sleep with her father that night the pilot whales beached. She reacted so strangely that I felt something was wrong. She didn't want to sleep with her father while I was in the house, because she was afraid I'd find out. She was afraid even more bad things would happen if anybody found out. You know, Anna?" Her voice went up.

"You know why I want to get to the bottom of this? When I saw Tara, it was as if I was looking at myself. She looked like a picture from my childhood. She talked like me, and was as angry as I was. I recognized her signals almost immediately.

"It only happened to me twice. And it was a friend of my parents whom I saw frequently, not my father. But it was horrible and as a child I didn't know what to do. I felt so dirty, so dirty!" The muscles in her neck began to move. Then all of the muscles in her face jumped. For a moment, I thought she'd burst out in laughter, but I was wrong. She cried with a dry sob, and without tears.

"I couldn't talk about it then. I thought I'd been so bad that everybody who'd hear it would hit me," she said when her voice had recovered. "When I was fourteen, I told my mother everything. But during the days that followed, I got so scared that the man would come to get me one night, that I took my words back and said I'd made up the whole thing. Now I've learned to talk about it. I can talk about all the details without it hurting me."

"Don't tell me," a little bird yelled in my head. "I don't want to listen." I don't know whether she told her entire story then, because I'd decided I didn't want to hear it. I only heard her voice again when she said:

"What does make me cry is that it happened to Tara. I can feel it — feel who it is. It's her father. She loves him. She trusts him. Can you understand it, Anna? You're still young, of course. I shouldn't have told you all this, because you'll get scared." She sniffed and took a sip of her coffee. I wished I had a bottle of perfume to hold under my nose.

"Tara has the same problem as Baby: when somebody touches her, it hurts. Out of shame, she can't grow anymore. She can only be scared of the horrible things that'll happen if she says anything." Through the window, Petr'Ann watched Tara move with her wet T-shirt over her body.

"That's why I thought: I can bring those two together. They'll understand each other. They both lost their mothers and share a lot of grief. I couldn't think of another solution for Baby. I'd tried everything. It was a gamble."

"Look!" I said softly after a minute, long silence. I stretched out my arm and my index finger and pointed toward the pool. "He's eating from her hand again." Petr'Ann nodded without looking up and went over to the table for more coffee.

"Thanks, Anna," she said as she poured. "Maybe you should go into the water one more time, otherwise Tara will start to ask questions."

When I slid into the pool, I saw Tara look at me curiously. The water hadn't been this cold before. My legs turned into icicles, and then my stomach and shoulders. Something in the water sucked me down, and it took minutes before I surfaced, gasping for air. I sat down on the side of the pool, my teeth chattering from the cold.

"I can't do it," I said to Petr'Ann who immediately came to my side. Tara swam over as well. Before she could reach me, I jumped up and walked head down to the change room. I didn't look into her eyes for a second.

27

That night, it seemed as though my body melted away into a bath of boiling water. I got very hot, and couldn't stop sweating. My sheets got wet, and I got really cold. The caretaker's little girl played her flute for hours. The monotonous sound hurt the muscles in my arms, my legs and my back.

"Anna can't come today," I heard distantly. It was light already. "She's sick. Here, Anna, drink this." Something tasted sweet and sour at the same time.

"I put the phone next to your bed. Here's the number. Call us if you have to. Caitlin promised to check in on you every hour."

"Caitlin?" I heard Tara say.

"The caretaker's little girl," Petr'Ann answered. "The doctor's coming around noon." I nodded with my eyes closed. I couldn't breathe through my nose, and my throat was as raw as a rasp. I slept and the only thing that woke me up was a thin little face peeping in and disappearing when I opened my eyes. Her ball on the floor below seemed to bounce around inside my skull.

When she came in the second time, she asked, "Do you want anything?"

"Water," I said, and took a few sips. Then I slept.

The heat woke me up. I looked at the islands on the wallpaper and thought about the dolphins. Tara and Petr'Ann were in the care pool together, and maybe Petr'Ann would say, "Anna told me everything yesterday. That's how I know about it."

"That witch!" Tara would answer. "She'll end up in a correctional institute if she doesn't keep her mouth shut." Tara and Petr'Ann plotted amongst themselves. They laughed, and dove into the water.

"Anna's easier to talk to, but you and I experienced the same thing," yelled Petr'Ann. "That makes us best friends."

I tried to concentrate on something else. "How many steps would the longest staircase in the world have?" I asked myself. There was a dead moth on the windowsill. I tried to cross my eyes while holding them closed, but it gave me a headache.

I imagined that I changed into boiling lava. I bubbled and sputtered up hot mud. The air bubbles in my stomach splashed open and smelled like sulphur. Lava poured out of my head onto the bed, off the bed, onto the carpet, down the stairs to the street. More and more lava came out, and after a while the entire room was filled higher than the windows. The windows burst under the pressure, and all of Boston flooded.

"She has a fever," an unfamiliar voice said. "Definitely stay in for three days. Probably just a flu, but take care of it."

"She has to go home the day after tomorrow. She lives in Cape Cod." That was Petr'Ann.

"If you dress her warmly before she gets in the car, she'll be all right. Give her lots to drink. No milk. Give her herbal tea or pop if she asks for it." They left the room and stayed away for a while. When Petr'Ann came back I said, "I want a Coke."

I stayed in bed the rest of that day and the next day too. Now and then, Petr'Ann and Tara came to report on the events in the pool. Baby let Tara ride on his back. They had placed a small transmitter on his dorsal fin, so they could follow him later in the open water. They'd finally been able to take blood samples again. And all because Tara had calmed him down. They didn't have the results of the blood tests yet, but if everything worked out, Baby would be ready to go into the ocean. They brought a small radio for me in case I got bored.

Tara felt sorry for me that I was missing all the fun.

"You should wet your hair and walk in the wind when you have a fever," she said.

"Tara!" Petr'Ann yelled. "What kind of nonsense is that! That's exactly what you shouldn't do." Tara started to laugh.

"I know that," she said. "My grandfather once told my dad that nonsense when he was sick. My dad did it, and my grandfather thought it was a great joke. Dad says he got quite sick then. He didn't have a mother, you see, and my grandfather did the craziest things to his son." I could tell by Petr'Ann's frown that she didn't think it was a funny joke.

That night, Tara sat beside me and ran her fingers through my hair. It was the first time she had done that and it felt nice. She didn't say much, and she was calm.

"I'm not afraid to go home," she said. "I'll just tell him, I don't want to do it anymore. Petr'Ann says she'll help me." She got undressed for bed as I watched.

Before we drove back to Cape Cod with Robert, Petr'Ann took me to the aquarium one last time. Tara was in the water, and demonstrated how Baby pulled her while she held on to his dorsal fin. The water splashed up, and she let out little screams of delight.

"Look!" Petr'Ann said right by my ear, and pointed at a sloppy wet pile beside the pool. It was the white T-shirt Tara had borrowed from me a few days before.

Tara got dressed, and walked down with me so we could watch the animals underwater one more time through the tall windows. Baby floated with his nose against the glass, and followed Tara when she walked back and forth along the window. They played hide and seek together, with Tara hiding behind the wall, and reappearing when Baby least expected it.

"We have to go," Robert said. I went over to him while Tara lagged behind a bit. From the benches I could overhear Petr'Ann, Roy and Robert speaking and I toyed with pulling my scarf over my nose and ears to amuse myself.

"I'll ask Tara's father to let her come a few more times. A matter of staying familiar with each other." Robert nodded.

"She can get a ride with me," he said.

"The girls should come along on the Albatross IV. They deserve it, and it could help Baby to have Tara around."

"Are you sure you want to do that?" Roy asked. "We'll follow the animals for three whole days, and that could get difficult. We don't have to take on any extra loads." Petr'Ann raised herself on her toes, which made her a lot taller than both men.

"I know why I'm doing this, Roy."

"Okay then, you're responsible," he said.

"Don't worry."

I felt as if butterflies were fluttering around my heart. I couldn't believe we were going to be allowed to come on the boat trip. Petr'Ann walked over to me and didn't mention it. She gave me a hug goodbye, and hugged Tara with a lot of whispering that I couldn't understand.

"See you soon," she said mysteriously.

I almost suffocated in the jeep, because I wanted to tell Tara about the boat trip. Robert acted as if nothing was going on. After a while, my back began to get warm again. My hands felt like rubber gloves that had been filled with hot water for a joke. My head tumbled against Tara's shoulder, and I slept.

Robert drove right up to our house, and he and Tara helped me out of the jeep. He talked to Mom and Dad briefly, and walked back to his car.

"See you later," he said. As soon as his jeep drove away, I pulled Tara with me and told her everything about the boat trip. She let out a deep yodel and danced around me.

"Well, Anna," Dad yelled from the other side. "You don't look that sick." Then we went inside.

28

I was sick for a while, and Mom told me I had to stay in my room, because I was contagious. I guess she wanted to keep me away from the bustle in the house.

The phone rang off the hook. Once it was Petr'Ann from Boston who talked to Mom and sometimes Dad for hours. There were people sitting in our kitchen whose voices and footsteps I didn't recognize. When I asked Mom who they were, she said they came to discuss insurance, or to sell books.

Mom walked through the house like a zombie. She did come to sit with me quite often, and made popcorn and brought bottles of Coke, but I noticed her blank gaze and incoherent train of thought.

"Can I watch TV downstairs tonight?"

"Mmmm?"

"Can I watch TV downstairs tonight?" I repeated, trying to be patient.

"TV? Maybe," she said. She didn't think about it for a second. That was obvious. That evening, she asked in complete surprise, "What are you doing down here in front of the television?"

During the late afternoon, I could hear Dad carrying on in the kitchen downstairs.

"That grease ball," he yelled a few times. And then, "How could we not have noticed? I'll never forgive myself. He better have left Anna alone." On the third day, Petr'Ann suddenly stood in my room. I was doing a puzzle.

"You look better," she said. I tugged the sheet over my right arm, because there was a hole in my pyjama sleeve. She brought me a book, called *My Life With Dolphins*.

"Have you seen Tara?" she asked.

"Mom doesn't want her to come over. She says I'm contagious."

"Your mom probably doesn't want you to know what's going on around here," she said loudly. I leafed through the book. Actually, I was glad Mom had shut me out. I didn't want to hear all the whispering and those secret stories about Uncle Tony. Just thinking about it made me gag.

"Tara's coming to Boston with me. She's going to do some therapy, which means that some people will talk with her, and help her find a solution for her problem. She's downstairs and wants to say goodbye to you after." Petr'Ann got up.

"Are you leaving already?" I asked.

"I'm in a hurry. I have to get back to the dolphins. I'm a bit of a mother, know what I mean?"

When Tara came to say goodbye, she hardly said anything. Like before, she was back in her glass tube from where she didn't hear anything and only watched. Her eyes were big and her eyelashes long. As she was leaving, I whispered, "I'll see you on the boat. Don't tell anybody we know. It's a secret, a secret like before, you know?"

She shut the door. I could tell by the way she talked to Petr'Ann that she was having trouble holding back her tears.

I stayed in my room a few more days with the sound of a baseball game in the background. I got used to the excited voice of the commentator, and slept right through it. When I was awake, I imagined uncle Tony sitting in his beach house like a hibernating animal waiting for his cat to come home. Deep inside me, a bear started to rummage wildly. He roared and tore out clumps of grass. I clenched my fists. I could only think of Uncle Tony as a nice uncle who changed into a sinister sneak at night, who silently lay down beside girls and made them cry with his sweet words.

When I was finally allowed to go outside, I walked to the beach house. The windows were covered with newspaper, and in front of the house there was a sign: HOUSE FOR RENT. I peered inside to make sure Uncle Tony wasn't sneaking around, with a present, or with one of Frank Sinatra's tunes coming out of his mouth. All the furniture was still there. There was even a bike with sand on its tires leaning against the oak cupboard. I heard the phone ring, but the hole in the front door had been closed off a long time ago, and I couldn't get in to answer. The ringing stopped and I walked back home. Mom didn't ask where I'd been.

"Shoes off! They're covered in sand!" she yelled. I nosed through the paper for news items about whales and dolphins. Especially for news that read: "Pilot whales set free off the Albatross IV. The operation headed by biologist Petr'Ann Jorssen became a success with the help of young Tara Myrold. The animals have completely adjusted to the ocean, and Ms. Jorssen is enjoying a well-deserved rest."

"I miss Tara," I told Mom, and she started talking about David. I went to my room and drank a glass of water in front of the mirror. I'd learned that from Tara. Drinking in front of a mirror is a strange experience. You can see your neck muscles move, your esophagus goes up and down and it all happens really quickly and automatically. Sometimes we stood in front of the mirrors in the beach house together until we burst out in laughter and the mirrors were dripping with pop.

I went downstairs again and finally summoned the courage to ask, "Where's Uncle Tony?" I asked softly because I was afraid he'd walk through the side door at the mention of his name, with his cowboy boots and bandanna, and with a nice smile. The night before, I'd dreamt he approached me with flowers in his arms, and then scratched my thighs and my back with his nails.

Mom looked away from me.

"He was taken away. He'd done something really bad." I could feel her prepare for the question that just had to come next — "What kind of bad thing, Mom?" but I didn't ask her, because I didn't really want to hear the story.

David came to see me with some homework, because I was no longer contagious.

"Have they moved?" he asked, and pointed through the window to the beach house.

"Yes," I said. "To Boston."

At school, no one said a word about Tara. First, the news had gotten out, and then the kids had spontaneously decided it was something they would never talk about. A little boy had taken her seat in the bus. Her work had been taken down from the walls in her classroom.

A week after she left, Tara called me.

"Anna, are you feeling better?"

I couldn't reply right away when I heard her. "Yes, I'm back at school."

"Have you read the book?" she asked.

"Yes, it was interesting. It's mainly about tumblers. It has pictures of a birth."

"I've read it. Petr'Ann has a copy on her shelf."

"How's Baby?"

"Fine. He plays with Tag and Notch again. Notch was a bit lazy today, but Petr'Ann says that's not a problem."

"Are you living with Petr'Ann now?"

"Yes, I see a therapist who works not far from here. I talk to Kim every day, always about the past, about what games I played and which books I read, and about what I feel and things like that. I have to draw too. It's just like kindergarten — a bit silly sometimes, but kind of fun too."

"Are you going to school in Boston?"

"I won't be going to school for a while, until I'm ready."

"Where's — your father?" That last word was hard to say. I was afraid she'd talk a lot about him, and I didn't want to hear anything about him. But I was curious about where he was.

"He's in Boston too. I only see him in therapy. We talk while Kim listens. Sometimes she asks a question, or sometimes she videotapes everything and we watch it afterward. Dad has to draw too. We're not allowed to have any contact without Kim around."

"We're working on a group drawing at school. The topic's 'the future,'" I said brightly but Tara wasn't listening.

"At night, he goes to a place called the Annex. He's there with all kinds of men who have the same problem." I didn't want to talk about this but she kept on. "It's not a prison. They can't just leave whenever they want, but there are no guards. It's more of a group home. He's allowed to do a lot of things, but he's not allowed to call me."

I could just imagine Uncle Tony in his James Dean shirt amongst a bunch of tough men with similar pasts. He would have his Walkman on, listening to Frank Sinatra. His head would be moving to the music. Nobody would talk to him, but he would smile at everybody anyway. "Real Man!" he would groan from time to time.

"When we're with Kim, he talks a lot about his past, and about his mother."

"I have to go now," I said quickly. "I think...somebody's... at the door and Mom's not here."

"Okay, I'll phone sometime." The line clicked. A plane flew over our house, low enough for me to think that it was about to burst through the window.

29

Tara phoned me every day. She told me about the pilot whales and about therapy. Wednesdays, she saw Uncle Tony. Wednesdays, I listened to the strangest stories about him.

"Dad's mother died when he was two. He never knew her. He remembers walking through the fields as a child, calling 'Mom!' because he didn't understand why she was gone. One time, he got lost in the fog. When they found him, he'd turned blue from the cold."

"Little Filip," I thought, but didn't say anything.

"He missed his mother very much. His father was mean to him. When they played soccer, he'd always kick the ball away from him until he cried and swore he'd never play again. Then Dad would go upstairs to listen to his mother's records. He'd eat after everybody had left the table. He'd sleep during the day and wander through the streets at night.

"Dad says I look like his grandmother. I guess he realizes now that what he did to me was wrong. He already knew that, but couldn't help it, he says. Remember we were so surprised I was allowed to go to Boston last month? Just yesterday he said, 'I let her go because I knew things were wrong. I couldn't leave her alone when she was near me. That's why I sent her away.' Don't you think that's weird, Anna?"

Yes, I thought it was weird, extremely weird. Horrible too. I wished she'd finally stop talking about it and let me talk for a bit. "I won a prize for an essay," I said.

"Really? What was it about?"

"About Boston and the aquarium, of course."

"Will you send me a copy?"

I promised to, and then said goodbye. The next day she

phoned again. She talked in detail about Baby and about swimming with him every day.

"He really knows me now!" she said proudly. He was making progress every day. Petr'Ann went out of her way to get everything ready for the transfer to the ocean. She did all kinds of complicated things that Tara and I didn't understand. The only thing we remembered was that the animals were all getting transmitters on their dorsal fins, so that through satellites their travelling routes could be traced for a while. We also knew the boat would follow the pilots for a while after unloading them, to see whether they would adjust to their new freedom.

"Do you know anything more about the boat?"

"Petr'Ann will phone you, don't worry. It won't be long. She can't help being so busy."

When the phone rang the next day, I thought it would be Tara. Dad got to the phone before I did.

"It's not Tara. It's somebody for me. Go back upstairs," he whispered. I left the living room but stayed by the door. Now and then I heard "I see…" and "Okay, I'll tell her." A little later, Dad called my doctor. He spoke even more softly.

"Isn't it too early for that?" he asked. And then: "No, no, I was only worried about her getting sick again while she's gone." After that, there was silence.

"There's a doctor on board, yes. Okay, she'll be happy. I wish I could come too." Thrilled, I snuck up the stairs and started to pack.

"Anna," Dad said after dinner. "Anna, come and sit with me. I want to tell you something." He laughed mysteriously. I sat down on the couch, and put my hand in his.

"Can I guess?" I said.

"You'll never guess it."

"It floats on water," I said.

"Why?"

"There are fish inside."

"What are you talking about?"

"I know it! I know it!"

Mom smiled in surprise. "What do you mean, you know it? You can't know it. I just heard myself."

"Okay, so I don't know it. Then tell me. What is it?"

"Then you *do* know it!"

"You just said I don't know it. Which is it?"

"Do you know something about a boat?"

"You mean the Albatross IV?" I asked innocently.

"By golly!" Dad yelped, and he slapped my thigh. "How did you know that? Petr'Ann assured me she hadn't told you and Tara anything."

"Walls have ears, remember?" I said. He always used to say that to Mom.

"Do you know that it's for a few days?"

"Yes, I know." His eyes looked like pingpong balls.

"Well, then I might as well not say anything else. I might as well be quiet."

"Just tell me where and when. That's all."

"Friday, ten o'clock, Boston," he said.

"Friday!" I shouted as loud as I could. Friday was a school day.

"You'll get behind in your studies. But I talked to your principal, and she understands. I told her you'd learn things on that boat you could never learn in school." I gave him a hug. He held me tight, and it felt nice.

He made me promise a few things about behaviour and politeness. About being quiet and unobtrusive. If I got seasick, I was go to my cabin, take some pills and wait until I got better. If I got a headache again, I was to see the doctor right away.

"Don't cause Petr'Ann any trouble. It'll be hard enough for her." I promised sincerely. I didn't let go of his hand all evening.

30

It seemed to take forever to get to Friday. At school, I watched the first spring rain create a swishing curtain in front of the window.

"Mom will be putting all of her plants outside," I thought. It got dark in the classroom, and somebody got up to switch the light on.

After school, I went for walks with my boots on. I walked to the playground with the wooden climbing racks and the swings. I used to come and play here years ago. There were gigantic puddles underneath the seesaws. The sand was beginning to smell like shells and pine needles again. There was nobody in the playground. The kids were still inside. How long until Friday?

On Thursday night, I knew I wouldn't be able to sleep. I set Mom's alarm clock up on my bedside, but I was afraid the power would go off with those squalls.

"I'll arrange a wake-up call if you're that worried," Dad teased. The whole evening, I watched the dial of the alarm. I had been reading in the sun for the first time that day, and my cheeks and forearms were glowing. Is Tara as nervous as I am? Is she lying there with eyes open wide watching the islands on the wallpaper? Is Baby ready to make the dangerous trip to the ocean?

At the first buzz of the alarm, I was awake. I'd dreamt, but couldn't remember what. Half an hour later, Robert was at the door. He carried a flashlight, because it was still dark outside.

"Good morning," he said much too loudly for the hour. "Are you up to it today?" Within ten seconds, I had my coat on. Dad carried my bag to the door wearing just his underwear.

"Don't let the sharks tear you to pieces," he joked, and gave me a kiss.

"Give that note to the doctor as soon as you board, that way you won't forget," Mom told me for the thirteenth time. She kissed me. I picked up my bag. It was heavier than it should be, because it had a few books "for when we got bored on the boat." Filed in between the books was an old card I'd found in my junk pile the day before. It was the card with the rainbow on it. I'd bought it at Thom Klika's a long time ago. Robert took my bag.

Gerd, the dune warden, sat behind the steering wheel, and there was a boy in the back seat.

"This is my son Alex," Gerd said. "Alex, this is Anna. She was one of the first to see the beaching." Alex made some room for me to get in.

"Did you swim with the pilots?"

"Yes," I nodded. "I and somebody else."

"Lucky," he sighed. "What an adventure! I'd give any money to do that." The beam from the headlights glided across our front door, the garage, the pine trees. The next moment, we were driving on the paved road, destination Boston.

"Do you want some M&Ms?" Alex asked. He rattled a few into my hand. I savoured them so long that they melted in my palm. I didn't have a Kleenex, so I licked the chocolate off while he wasn't looking.

"Tell me about the aquarium," he said. I shrugged my shoulders.

"What do you want to know?" I said.

"Everything. What do they eat? What kind of sounds do they make?"

"They make a lot of different noises. Sometimes they sound like a squeaking door that opens and closes, and sometimes like a woodpecker. They eat fish — mostly squid."

"How fast do they swim?"

"I don't know."

He wanted to know the most impossible things. The size of the pool, water temperature, salt content of the water, filtration system.

"Alex, leave the girl alone," Gerd called to the back. "Not

everybody's as crazy about numbers as you are." He glanced at me in the rearview mirror.

"Don't let him, Anna," he said. "Alex just wants to test you. He knows the answers to all his questions." Robert and Gerd started to laugh. Alex grinned at me. He gave me some more M&Ms. Later, the constant zooming by of trees and houses, and Alex's sleepy head bobbing up and down, was making me sleepy. The next thing I remember is that it was completely light and Boston was before us.

Gerd drove us to the quay where the Albatross IV was docked. Then he pulled away to park his jeep in the aquarium's parking lot. With my bag in my arms, I followed Robert and Alex and boarded the ship. All kinds of people were walking back and forth, all of them unfamiliar faces. Robert didn't quite know where to go either. I looked for something red moving around. The gulls screamed above our heads, and I smelled hay.

"Anna!" hollered Tara.

"Tara!" She jumped on my back and threw her arms around my neck. I dropped my bag to the ground.

"Petr'Ann! Anna's here. And Robert."

"This is Alex," I said. "The dune warden's son."

"Hi," she said without looking at him. "Anna, come. The animals will be loaded on soon. It's so exciting. Petr'Ann didn't sleep a wink last night."

Alex watched her. He watched her long eyelashes like a biologist, and smiled somewhat startled when Robert started to talk to him.

Petr'Ann appeared with a bucket of squid in each hand. She put the buckets down and hugged me.

"You smell like fish," I said.

"And you smell like Cape Cod," she laughed. She went on, and Tara followed her. Some people on board carried complex photography equipment. They took shots of Boston and the sea ducks.

"Come on Anna, I'll show you our cabin," Tara called out. Alex rushed over to her.

"Do you know where I'm supposed to sleep?"

"Of course. Come along!" I almost got stuck in the narrow hallways with my bag. Tara showed Alex and Gerd their cabin.

"And this is ours," she said. The walls were covered with wood and fake leather.

"You brought your red dress?" I asked, when I saw the red clothing.

"Yes, Petr'Ann told me I'd need it," she answered. She hung the dress right at the back of the closet. I zipped open my bag and took out my books.

"Wow, you're going to read all those?" Tara said. She showed me where the sinks were. Then she took me to the lunch room and Petr'Ann's cabin.

"Cozy," I kept saying. We bumped into a woman coming down the stairs with blood samples in her hand.

"Hurry to the deck. The animals are being loaded on," she said.

Alex came over to us while we watched. Notch was hanging in a special kind of hammock on the nose of a gigantic crane. He didn't move, but watched us with one eye. On the deck, there were three polyester tanks half filled with water.

"There's a thick layer of foam at the bottom, to prevent too much pressure on their intestines," Tara informed us. "Petr'Ann told me," she added immediately. I saw Alex stare at her eyes. Notch reached the water. The crane no longer made that creaking noise.

"Now he's half in the water," Tara said. It reached just above his side fins.

"Why don't they fill the tanks up a bit more?" I asked.

"When the boat rocks, the water splashes up. Notch could choke himself if his spout hole filled up."

"How long can pilots survive that way?" Alex asked. He went to stand next to her and leaned over the railing. I went to the bathroom.

I stood in front of the small square mirror and licked my fingers. I curled my eyelashes out with my spit. They got a little darker because of the moisture, but they remained thin and blond. It was too bad I hadn't brought Mom's mascara.

"See that red little thing attached to their dorsal fin?" Tara asked when I'd returned. "That's the transmitter. That's how the biologists always know exactly where they are. It's interesting to find out which routes they take, and why." It was Tag's turn. It was strange to see this powerful giant hanging in the stretcher so helplessly. She was so elegant in the water, and here looked so heavy and still.

"They'll be lonely in the ocean," I said. "They've always lived in a pod of at least fifty animals, and during the past few months there were always people playing games with them."

"My dad said there's a real possibility they'll die," Alex said. "He also said they might meet a pod of pilot whales or other dolphins," he added quickly. "Apparently, pods sometimes adopt lonely animals."

To me his words sounded like a fun idea for a Walt Disney movie. Tara shook her head.

"They'll probably be on their own for the rest of their lives," she said. She suddenly turned around and went to our cabin. Alex watched her leave in surprise.

After Baby had been hoisted aboard, the ocean started to foam at the bow.

"We're leaving."

"Anna, where's Tara?" Petr'Ann asked. "Oh, there she is." Tara joined us again.

"Isn't sailing fun!" Petr'Ann said. "I used to sail with my father and grandfather, or with a friend of my parents who was a fisherman too. They sailed through the Scheldt to the North Sea."

"The Scheldt," Tara echoed.

"Sailing out was always a very important moment. Sailing out determined whether you'd come home safely."

"How's that?" Alex asked. He leaned sideways to listen to Petr'Ann. His sleeve touched my arm.

"There were a lot of things that brought bad luck. To meet a black cat, a nun or a priest before sailing out was said to bring bad luck. Killing an albatross was fatal too. If somebody wished you a safe trip, you'd definitely go down, or if somebody on the boat spilled salt. You weren't allowed to whistle, because the wind would die down, and then you wouldn't be going anywhere. You weren't allowed to mend clothes on deck either, because the fishermen believed you'd sew up the wind." Petr'Ann greeted a man passing by.

"Anna, that's the doctor. You can give him your mother's note later," she said. I promised I would.

"Tell us more," Tara said impatiently.

"There were also things that brought good luck," Petr'Ann started again. "If you threw a coin overboard, you could buy the wind. Or you could put a coin under the mast, so you wouldn't lose it."

"Let's do it!" Tara yelled. "Let's put a coin under the mast."

"There is no mast," Alex said dryly.

"Then we'll throw one overboard." Alex flamboyantly took out his wallet and gave her a quarter. She threw the coin as far as she could into the water.

We'd been sailing for a few hours, when the skipper suddenly started to shout.

The word "dolphins" travelled from mouth to mouth. I'd seen something move for a while already, but hadn't said anything because I wasn't sure what it was. Soon we saw bigger shapes pushing through the water.

"That's a humpback — it's a whale too," Robert said. "And look over there, that's a fin fish, way in the distance. Look how incredibly big it is."

"You can hardly see him," Tara protested.

"I recognize them by their backs and the way they spout," Robert said. The dolphins nearby shot through the water like arrows. After a long wait, we got closer to the humpbacks and fin fish. They made a lot of noise, like vacuum cleaners that sometimes don't get enough power. They watched us as curiously as we watched them.

Gerd went over to Alex.

"See him watching," he said, as he pointed to the small eye of the humpback. "He says, 'Maybe you read a human book about whales, but I read a whale book about humans.' What do you think?" Alex forced himself to laugh at his dad's joke.

"Bad joke," he said. Then he asked Tara, "Does your dad tell jokes as bad as that?" Tara didn't say anything. Gerd pretended not to have heard his son's comment.

"Humpbacks have an extremely sophisticated communication system. They used to be able to chat with each other from one side of the ocean to the other. With all the navigation and drilling in the ocean floor that has become impossible, because there are too many disturbing noises. All that noise must be nervewracking when your hearing is that sensitive."

The ocean was getting rougher. My stomach felt a bit funny, but I didn't mention it to anyone.

"There's quite a variety of whales here," Robert said. Gerd nodded confirmingly.

"This corner is famous for that, just like Cape Cod. There's whale watching here too. It's very expensive, but if you don't see any whales, you get your money back." A man who looked like a real fisherman joined them. I nudged Tara and pointed at his arm. It had a tattoo of a mermaid tied to a pole. Her breasts were bare and her face looked distorted. Tara started to giggle.

"Is that Goody Hallett?" she asked shamelessly. The fisherman looked at his arm.

"Goody Hallett?" he asked. "Goody Hallett. You mean that seawitch that makes the Cape Cod guys pee their pants?"

"Why's she tied up?"

"What do I know?" the fisherman asked, and walked away.

31

"A pod of pilot whales!" Robert pointed out, his voice shrill with excitement. Suddenly, the deck was crowded with people. Petr'Ann disappeared in a flash. Everybody ran around and screamed. The boat seemed to rock even more. Roy Prescott yelled something at us, but I couldn't hear what, because of the loud wind. I saw a group of men clustering around the tanks.

"Notch goes first," somebody standing close to me said. The group pushed an odd-looking cage with a sliding bottom underneath Notch.

"They'll keep each animal in the cage until it's used to the water," Alex said, having heard that from his father. Tara told him she already knew that. I think it was Bert who attached the cage to the crane.

"Lift!" yelled Roy Prescott.

"Hurry!" Tara grumbled. "The pod's leaving." The chains on the crane tightened. Notch was slowly lifted off the deck, then moved horizontally until he dangled above the water. His transmitter was placed at the front of his dorsal fin.

"Down!" Roy Prescott yelled. From that point on, things went wrong. The ocean was too rough. The cage wobbled a lot and almost tilted. The chain came undone. Notch dropped like a boulder into the water, cage and all. The meshes snapped, the cage banged open, the transmitter caught on a piece of rope.

Roy cursed loudly, and Alex mumbled, "Dammit, this shouldn't have happened." But Notch didn't seem to be wounded. He calmly started to swim around. Everybody mumbled and had an opinion.

"The transmitter," the voices said. "The transmitter has come off. How horrible for Roy and Petr'Ann. All those preparations for their shark research." Notch swam to the other side of the boat.

"Why don't they numb him out and attach the transmitter again?" I asked Tara. I immediately realized that that wouldn't work.

"I thought you knew whales breathe consciously. If you make them unconscious, they drown." I was glad Alex hadn't heard my question. He was watching the crane being repaired. Tag and Baby had to stay on board until things were less rough. And Notch disappeared all by himself, without showing any interest in the vanishing pod of whales.

By early evening, everything was ready to lower the other two pilot whales into the water. The ocean had calmed down. We hadn't seen Notch all afternoon, but he appeared in the distance as if he sensed that Tag and Baby would soon join him.

"It's Notch. He's found us again!" Tara yelled, because she recognized him before anyone else on board.

"He probably follows the sound of the Albatross," Robert said. "It's unbelievable what kind of memory those animals have."

Tag and Baby were lowered into the water one after the other. It was a strange spectacle: a silhouette of fish dangling from a crane slowly falling toward the water with the sunset as a backdrop. Their tails moved up and down a few times before they disappeared into the water completely. They dove down and surfaced excitedly.

At first, they swam back and forth wildly, but after a while they relaxed. A group of dolphins came to check out what was going on in the twilight, and circled around the pilots. There was an echo of clicking and whistling noises.

"Their communication system is unsurpassable," Robert started again. "They can speak on two levels simultaneously: they exchange information by whistling, and simultaneously by clicking. It's as if we could speak Chinese and English at the same time."

"They're telling them what happened in the ocean during their absence," Tara fantasized.

"And the pilots are telling them about the care pool in Boston, and about those two wonderful girls they met," I added. She burst out laughing.

"Don't exaggerate, Baby," Tara called out. "One of them was wonderful, but the other one was a monster," she said in a fake voice. I playfully nudged her between the ribs. She grabbed my arm and took me to Petr'Ann who was talking to a journalist.

"I'm quite satisfied. Everything went reasonably well, although losing Notch's transmitter is very disappointing. But at least, Baby and Tag still have theirs, and that's something," she said. Then she saw us and said, "Oh, these two have to be in the article too. They helped a lot."

Tara had to talk about her adventures with Baby, and we got our picture taken. The flash hurt my eyes.

Alex was still watching the water.

"It's gotten very dark. Hopefully they won't get lost," I said, jokingly because I wasn't really worried.

"The ocean's full of roads," Alex said wisely. "There are highways that all whales can perceive, but no human can see, because we don't have the right senses. Because of those highways, they always know where they are." Robert came over.

"Sometimes something goes wrong," he added. "You could call it road disturbance. Then they beach. But, of course, you know all about that." It was getting chilly outside, and we went to our cabin. My back was sore from standing at the railing for so long.

"When I close my eyes, I can see the ocean," Tara said lying stretched out on her mattress.

"Come take my shoes off and wash me. I can't move anymore."

"No, you're taking my shoes off and bringing me a Coke. I'm really dead." We both took our shoes off and crawled underneath the blankets without bothering to change or wash.

It was very foggy on the second day, and we couldn't really see what was going on at sea. I hung around the machine room and watched Petr'Ann draw strange things with the computer.

"Anna, would you mind leaving? I have to concentrate," she said. The fisherman with the mermaid on his arm was cutting vegetables in the kitchen.

"Ah, madame from Cape Cod!" he called out boisterously when I entered. I asked him what he was cooking and he told me it was a surprise. Didn't I know there was a party tonight to celebrate the pilots' successful return to the ocean?

"Are we invited too?"

"Of course, the captain's inviting everybody." He waved his knife exuberantly. A piece of broccoli fell on the floor.

"Anyway," he added in a whisper. "We need more women to dance with, right? There aren't that many, and Ms. Jorssen's too tall for any of us. We'd need a ladder." He laughed loudly. I asked him for a glass of water and went upstairs.

"Do you want a sip?" I asked Tara who was all wrapped up in blankets, reading a book. She drank and handed the half-empty glass back to me.

"Is it cold on the deck?"

"Quite. There's a party tonight. We have to dance. Everybody's invited."

"Great," she said. "But I won't dance."

"Alex will dance with you," I said teasingly.

"Not over my dead body. That slime ball."

"Slime ball?" I said outraged. "I think Alex is a really nice guy."

"Are you going to dance with him?"

"I think I'm too shy," I said. "I want him to ask me, though."

"If he loves you, he'll ask you," she said. She read a few sentences in her book. Then she looked up at me again and whispered, "If he loves you, he'll put his hands between your legs." I just about choked. I started to cough loudly, put the glass down and walked to the bathroom. When I caught my breath, I didn't want to go back to the cabin. I never wanted to talk about boys to Tara again. When she talked about it, the light feeling in my stomach turned into something cold, something dirty, something bad and something secret.

Tara put her arm around my shoulders.

"Sorry I called him a slime ball," she said into my ear. "I didn't know you liked him." She sat down with me on the metal steps leading to the lunchroom. The cook slapped plastic plates on the table.

"Anna, I said I was sorry," she said urgently. "Why didn't you tell me earlier you had a crush on him? Or was it a secret?" I still didn't say anything. She put her hands on the back of my neck.

"Now I know a secret about you. That's what I wanted, right?" She massaged my shoulders until I was completely limp.

"Let's go to the cabin," she said. "It's cold on these steps." I got up and came with her. There was a book I wanted to read. I arranged my pillow against the wall, and made myself comfortable. When I opened my book, a card with a drawing of a rainbow fell out. I scratched the pink ribbon. Over the years, the smell had faded, and it smelled of fish more than strawberries. I turned the card over and wrote *for Tara, from Anna*. I got up and sat down on her bed.

"That's fun," she said.

"If you scratch it, you smell all kinds of fruit. Orange smells like oranges, purple like grapes, yellow like bananas and red like strawberries." She sniffed it and read the quote inside: TEARS DO FOR EYES WHAT A RAINBOW DOES FOR THE SKY.

"That's beautiful. What do you think it means?"

I shrugged my shoulders. "Maybe it means that it's good to cry sometimes. I'm not sure. Something like that."

She looked at me and said, "Were you crying before, in the bathroom?" I scratched my left palm and didn't answer.

"I never used to want to cry," she continued. "I thought it was childish. But everything made my head feel like it was full of water. It was so full, I couldn't think anymore and it made my eyes blurry. It felt as though one day my skin would explode and at least ten litres would pour out. One day, I couldn't keep it in anymore. It was because of something you'd said."

"What did I say?"

"Something mean."

"What was it? I don't remember anymore."

"You said, 'Now I understand why your mother committed suicide. Life must be Hell with a child like you.'"

"Oh yes, I remember. But that was because I was angry. I didn't really mean it."

"Anyway, I cried a lot that time. I really believed it was my fault then. I thought Mom swallowed all those pills to get rid of me. Kim claims that's where the problem lies. That I feel guilty about what happened. Do you think it's my fault?"

I didn't quite know how to answer.

"No," I said. "I think Aunt Tanja was like the pilot whales. She did it without anybody knowing why. Maybe she was lost too." Tara crawled against me.

"She didn't understand anything," she said in a harsh voice. "If I tried to tell her anything, she'd walk away. When I was a baby, she'd play a cassette with her voice on it beside my crib. Then she'd leave the house. I'd wake up in the dark and hear her soothing voice whisper, 'Hush now Tara-darling, hush' over and over again. But no matter how hard I cried, she never came." She grated her thumb knuckles along her teeth as she talked. Her story made my eyes burn.

"But you know," she said. "When the tears came, the words started to come too. It was the first time I said anything to you."

I remembered. I still remembered it all very clearly, and wished I didn't ever have to think about it again. I wished I was a seven-year-old child building sand castles with shell rooves and underground tunnels and real trees around the moat.

32

The party started with glasses of wine set out on a table. I was one of the first to get to the dining room, because the book was boring, and I had nothing else to do. I wore my flowered skirt that came to just above my knees and my special bracelet. The fisherman whistled when I entered the kitchen.

"Are there any snacks? Or chips?" I asked. He pointed at the anchovy on the counter.

"Here, why don't you take that," he said. When I got back to the dining room, more people had arrived. Roy carried a bag. A journalist was taking pictures.

"Looks great!" Petr'Ann said when she saw me. She was wearing makeup and held a glass in her right hand. "Is Tara not ready yet?"

"She's still getting changed," I said. I was hoping she wouldn't wear that beautiful red dress. It was a flowing dress with lace around the bottom. Just like one I'd been wishing for, for years. Her father had given it to her. In fact, I had been there when he'd said, "I chose red, because that's your favourite colour, right puss?"

A man with an accordion entered. A few people set up a microphone and speakers. Somebody turned off the neon lights and only left the little ones against the wall on. Yellow light flooded the room, and the music started.

"Hi," Alex said. "This will be fun, don't you think?" He smelled like soap and musk. I pointed out to him where the Coke was, but he said he wanted to wait a bit.

Tara entered through the side door. She wore her red dress. It closed on her neck and had little bands at the elbows. Her hair was combed back and tied in a ponytail. With her head slightly bent to one side, she came over to us.

"I've never worn this before. I feel so awkward," she whispered to me.

"Are you still afraid of Goody Hallett?" I whispered back. It sounded like a joke, but actually I wanted to hurt her. I felt like such a sap in my flowered skirt. Alex noticed her and immediately went over to her.

"That red looks really good on you," he said, and I stuffed my mouth with anchovy. The salt distorted my face. I went to the kitchen for a glass of water.

It took a while before people started to dance. They played songs everybody knew, and sometimes the accordion player played fishing songs. We teased Petr'Ann.

"Petr'Ann, did you bring your boyfriend?"

"Petr'Ann, do you have a boyfriend. What's his name? What does he look like?"

"He's big and strong," she said.

"Bigger than you, Petr'Ann?"

"Oh, much, much bigger. He has dark, soft skin and shining white teeth. He has small, dark eyes. He moves very elegantly. His favourite dish is squid, prepared with my recipe of course. He's very calm and doesn't get angry easily. What else? Oh yes: he's very athletic, too. He swims every day."

"Is he a good cook, Petr'Ann?"

"Mmmm, he's got some trouble with cooking."

"And where is he now?"

"Oh, I guess he went for a swim. We'll probably see him tomorrow. Then he'll come and tell me all about the tons of fish he's polished off, and what the ocean's like. Of course, he'll also tell me how much he loves me."

Alex was enjoying her story. He went to get some cookies and brought some for Tara too. He even sipped from her glass once. The cook brought out some sort of smoked mackerel which I tried and then spat into my hand. I wrapped up the awful thing in my serviette and threw it in an ashtray. The brown cigarette smoke made my eyes watery.

"Roy, do you smoke a pipe?" I heard Petr'Ann say. "Let's

share it to celebrate the whales." She sucked on it and then exhaled. The smoke came out of her mouth in circles.

"Mmm, tastes better than I thought," she said. The music was turned up, and Bert dimmed the lights by covering them with articles of clothing.

"Do you want to start a fire?" somebody shouted.

"Don't worry about it," he answered. More and more feet started to move to the music's rhythm. Tara put her cheek against my upper arm.

"Still a head taller than me. We'd make good dance partners."

The boat rocked a little. Apparently, the wind was picking up again. I thought about the three animals outside in the cold water of the Atlantic Ocean. We'd stopped following them a couple of hours ago. The research had been finished. It looked like there were no adjustment problems worth mentioning.

"I miss my dad," Tara interrupted my thoughts. "I feel so badly that he has to sit in the Annex by himself while I'm having such a fun time. I wish he were here."

I tried to imagine him here, eating mackerel, pulling his fingers until his knuckles cracked, asking the deejay to play a special request for his daughter — one of Sinatra's songs, no doubt.

"Tara, do you want to dance?" I heard Alex ask. She seemed to hesitate, but then went anyway. She made faces at me over his shoulder. I sat down at a table and watched them dance.

Her hands lay on his shoulders in the same way she had gingerly touched Baby a few weeks ago: only her palms brushed him, her fingertips were bent upward. She kept her head turned away from his, and there was an awkward gap between them.

"If Alex pulls her toward him now, she'll scream and run away," I predicted. But he didn't. He handled her as if he were dancing with a glass doll. Even when the music slowed down and the atmosphere became more intimate, they stayed far apart. It was a rare spectacle, he with his hand on her shimmering dress. It made me think of things I hadn't thought of for a long time.

Of a faded photograph of Tara with the glasses behind the cupboard in the garage, for example. Or of the walls of the beach house covered with drawings of fish and bottles. Of a glass of greenish lemonade without fizz on a boiling porch. Of a man and a woman with a knitted scarf on the beach. Of a wide wooden staircase with runners of a different brown than the wood underneath it. Of going swimming, and peeling the bathing suit off my body under a towel afterward, and finding sand in my belly button and ears. Of boys skateboarding over hills, down steps, on benches and through A.D. Makepeace's flower beds. Of a sign that said HOUSE FOR RENT.

The longer Tara danced, the more she blinked her eyes. Her eyes were searching for me, and she looked at me like a scared kitten. When the music died down, she tore herself away. She immediately came toward me.

"Was it fun?"

"I'm not dancing anymore," she said. "I don't like it."

"Why, he didn't..."

"He smells like onions," she said quickly, and left the room through the side door.

It took a long time before she returned. She came back in her torn jeans and faded T-shirt. Like a ghost, she moved behind people's backs to a place against the wall in a corner. Alex asked her something, but she shook her head.

"I wouldn't mind dancing with you, if Tara doesn't feel like it anymore," I said when he sat down beside me.

"I'll take a breather first," he said. Together we watched Tara. I thought: maybe all that pain will heal. Maybe, one day, she'll let herself be touched again, just like Baby. Petr'Ann sat at a table holding a glass of beer. She sucked on her pipe and smiled at Tara against the wall. Then, in one exuberant gulp, she polished off her beer.